SUNLIT SURRENDER

BANDICOOT COVE SERIES: A NOVELLA

SUNLIT SURRENDER

BANDICOOT COVE SERIES: A NOVELLA

JESS DEE

Entangled Publishing, LLC
2614 South Timberline Road
Suite 109
Fort Collins, CO 80525
Visit our website at www.entangledpublishing.com.

Scorched is an imprint of Entangled Publishing, LLC.

Edited by Jennifer Miller
Cover design by Heather Howland
Cover art from iStock

eBook ISBN 9781633759886
paperback ISBN 978-1546397885

Manufactured in the United States of America

First Edition September 2012
Second Edition June 2017

entangled
scorched

To Sami and Lex, for maintaining those impossibly high standards Kylie insists on, and for keeping the magic flowing through Bandicoot Cove.

With Thanks

*To Fedora, Dawn and Kitty Kelly. You are the bestest!
And, as always, to Jennifer, for once again joining us at
Bandicoot Cove—and for making everyone's trip here that
much more amazing.*

Chapter One

See Aidan
See McKenzie
See Aidan and McKenzie get married.

Dear Bianca Rogers,

Aidan and Mack would love to invite you and your "plus one" to bear witness to their wedding on Bandicoot Cove's main beach,

Saturday, four p.m.

Dress is completely casual as the atmosphere will be relaxed and full of laughter. No top hats, tuxedos or stilettos allowed.

Please come and share in Aidan and Mack's special day as they finally formalize what the rest of the world already knew: they were meant to be together from the start.

RSVP Kylie Sullivan
Bandicoot Cove Resort
Bilby Island, Australia

Bianca fingered the invitation with a sigh. "Plus one". Damn if those words didn't tear a hole through her heart. When had she ever needed a "plus one"?

Never, that's when.

She and Rick had been together since school, for heaven's sake. Since she was sixteen.

You're too young, they'd been warned countless times. *It'll never last.*

God, she hated those words.

At least wait until you've finished uni. Get your degrees.

They had gotten their degrees. Several years after their wedding.

She set the invitation on the glass table in the center of the luxurious living room. Maybe they should have waited. Maybe they had been too young. One thing was for sure. It hadn't lasted. Not long enough, anyway.

Which was why Kylie had addressed the invitation to Bianca Rogers. Per Bee's request, her married name had been dropped, and after ten years she'd reverted back to using her maiden name. Although the divorce wasn't final yet. Not until she and Rick had added their initials and signatures to the papers.

She'd sign them as soon as she got home. It was the top

item on her to-do list. Not now, though. Not while she was on this glorious tropical island. Now was not the time to mull over her life or her failed marriage. Now was not the time for regrets. It was a time for celebration and joy.

Bee shoved her feet into a pair of Havaianas and headed for Oasis, the resort's poolside bar. She had a meeting there in less than ten minutes with Mack—her sister-in-law-to-be, Kylie—Mack's BFF and Bandicoot Cove's manager, and the hotel photographer—Kennedy someone or other. If she didn't move her arse, she'd be late.

So determined was she to get to the bar on time, Bee almost tripped over a man as she hurried from her beautiful beachside bungalow and made her way through the lush gardens.

"Whoa. Easy there." Strong hands reached out to steady her.

Bee caught herself mid-stumble, grateful for the muscular arms that prevented her from falling. She looked up to say thank you and immediately lost her breath.

Try as she might, she could not remember the last time seeing a man had taken her breath away. But the second her gaze touched his face, there went her oxygen. Gone. Just like that.

"Are you okay?" His voice was soft, a whispered caress, although she was pretty sure that wasn't how he'd intended it to come across. He looked at her with concern, not blinding, unexpected lust.

It was she who was blinded by unexpected lust.

Dear Lord, he was gorgeous. Sexy, in a knock-your-socks-off kind of a way. Not classically good-looking. His nose was a little too crooked for that. And his lower lip a little too plump. Good for nibbling on, but not so good in front of a camera.

But then Bee never carried a camera with her, so that point was irrelevant. She did, however, carry her mouth around at all times, so a little nibble—the smallest taste of that lower lip—was a distinct possibility.

She knew how it would taste too. Sweet. Soooo sweet. With a hint of something unknown, mysterious. All wrapped up with a little dusting of spice. For added flavor.

Her mouth watered.

His eyes were an odd color. Neither blue nor green. More like a mixture of the two, the exact shade of the ocean behind her. Crystal clear and utterly beautiful. She kind of fancied she could read his every thought in them. And as soon as she'd decided she could, she decided not to try. Rather leave the mystery than try to understand him. Mystery was good.

Perhaps that was one of the problems between Rick and her. There'd been no mystery. They'd been together too long for that.

But if there'd been no mystery, how was it they'd become strangers?

She brought her attention back to the stranger standing before her. It was all Bee could do not to flip back the dark lock that fell over his forehead so endearingly. She wanted to run her fingers through his hair so badly, they actually itched.

His hands tightened around her arms. "Are you okay?" he repeated. "Winded?" Concern was replaced by worry. "Can you breathe?" He released one arm suddenly, holding her steady with the other, and brought his hand behind her back.

Dear Lord. Was he going to hug her?

A hug would be nice. Unexpected, but nice. Especially if she got to cuddle into that lovely chest of his. Big, but not too big. Solid and inviting…

That was what she'd always thought about Rick's chest. Big, lovely, solid and inviting. Even when he was a teenager.

He tapped her firmly on the back.

Ah, so not a hug. More like a halfhearted attempt at the Heimlich maneuver.

"It's okay," she piped up, remembering she not only had a voice, but lungs too, and was perfectly capable of using both. "I'm okay. I can breathe fine."

He immediately dropped his hand. It took him a little longer to release her arm though, and when he did, Bee almost complained. She liked the feel of his grasp there.

"I'm sorry." He offered an apologetic smile. "You had me worried. For a minute I thought you might be choking."

"Nope. Not choking. Just surprised." Very surprised. "I didn't see you." She wasn't sure how she'd missed him—since he towered above her. In fact, standing in front of him, she couldn't see anything else. He blocked her vision entirely.

She eyed him with speculation. Oh, he was sexy indeed. Sexy and gorgeous. He looked like her ideal man.

On impulse—because wasn't that the way she always did things, on impulse?—she stuck out her hand. "I'm Bianca, by the way. Bianca…" She struggled with her last name. "Rogers."

His jaw dropped.

His surprise kind of mirrored hers. Would it ever feel right using that name again? Introducing herself by it?

And then she couldn't concentrate on her name at all anymore because with his mouth open like that, the urge to nibble on his full bottom lip was overwhelming. She wondered if he'd mind if she stood on tiptoes, pulled his head close to hers and helped herself to a taste.

He probably would. Better to keep talking. "My friends call me Bee, though."

He stared at her for a long, silent minute.

Bee cleared her throat. "Uh, usually, at times like this, you'd introduce yourself. You know, tell me your name and all." *Flirting, Bee? Really?*

He raised an eyebrow. "My name?"

"Yeah. You know. It's the title your parents gave you when you were born. Helps other people to identify you."

He blinked once, as though startled, and then nodded slowly. "Ah, yes. My name. It's...Brody. Brody Evans." He stuck out his hand, and she slipped hers in it, loving the way his fingers curled around hers as they shook. So formal. So... tempting.

"So, Mr. Evans, are you here on the island alone?" Shameful of her to ask, but there'd be no point taking this any further if he wasn't.

Her heart shocked her then, racing overtime as she awaited his answer.

Nervous, Bee?

Er, yeah. Very. What if he is *here with someone?*

It would be crushing.

Brody hadn't released her hand. Instead he stared at it as though he'd never seen a hand before. Or maybe he was staring at the white band of flesh around her ring finger. She knew she stared at it a lot. Perhaps to the point of obsession. Not long ago a simple gold ring had covered it, but she'd removed that when the divorce papers arrived. No point wearing it anymore, now was there?

"I am," he answered eventually. "Well, kind of. I came

for a wedding. So I guess you could say I'm here with lots of people."

"Well, isn't that a coincidence? I'm here for a wedding too."

"Bianca…Rogers? Would I be right in assuming you're here for Mack and Aidan's wedding?"

She grinned at him. "You would indeed. Savvy mind you have there. Aidan's my brother. You here for the same wedding?"

He grinned back, and the sheer warmth in his smile heated her blood. It had been a long time since a smile had affected her like that. "I am."

"On the bride or groom's side?"

"The groom. Although I know the bride too. We all go back a long time."

It was her turn to look at him speculatively. "So you know the bride and groom, and you have for a while. It's interesting that we've…uh…never met before. I thought I knew all of Danny's mates."

Brody took a long time to answer. Once again, Bee fancied she might be able to read his thoughts in those beautiful eyes but immediately decided she had to be wrong.

"Are you sure we've never met?" he asked finally. "You look…familiar."

Bee shook her head. "Nope. I'd have remembered if we had. You're not the type of person one would forget in a hurry." He wasn't the type of person she'd forget ever.

He tilted his head to the side, regarding her thoughtfully. He opened his mouth to say something, must have thought better of it, closed it again, then said, "Would you like to have a drink with me, Bianca?"

And just like that, Bianca's mouth was drier that it had

ever been. Her throat was parched too, as though she hadn't had liquid in a year, at least. A drink with him was exactly what she wanted. Needed. "I'd love to."

His smile was blinding. "Excellent."

He gave her a swift once-over, making Bee instantly self-conscious. Wearing nothing but a bikini had seemed like a good idea in this heat, but having Brody's gaze—brief as it was—take in every inch of her lily-white skin was a little inhibiting.

"Looks like you're all ready for a swim," he said. "Tell you what, I need to change, put on a pair of boardies. How about I meet you at the poolside bar in…ten minutes?"

Ten minutes? That felt like a veritable lifetime. "Ten minutes would be perf— No, shoot!" Bianca slapped her forehead. "Sorry, sorry. It won't be perfect. I already have a meeting in ten minutes. Actually, more like one minute now, and if I'm late, Mack is gonna let me have it." More like Kylie was gonna let her have it. The woman ran a tight ship. Her only instruction to Bee had been not to be late.

Uh, yeah. About that…

"Look," she hastened to say, "I can't do drinks. How about lunch instead? They serve a killer salad nicoise at the Seaspray Bistro."

Brody wrinkled his nose at the very suggestion. "Tuna salad?"

She grinned at him. "Not a fan, huh? Me neither. But Mack's friend recommended it to me, so I thought I'd recommend it to you."

"How about a simple grilled cheese sandwich and a bottle of red wine instead?"

Bee's jaw dropped. She couldn't help it.

She and Rick had shared that exact meal on the night

of their wedding. In the cheap hotel they'd chosen for their honeymoon. Gourmet food it hadn't been, but Bee had never eaten anything more delicious.

She swallowed at the memory. "G-grilled cheese sounds really good."

"To me too." His smile was warm, but his eyes…

"Shall we say twelve thirty? At a table outside?" Aidan was arriving on the island then, so Mack would ensure they'd be done by that time.

"I'll be waiting for you."

As Bee waved goodbye and headed off to her meeting, she couldn't help but think how incredibly appealing the idea of Brody Evans waiting for her sounded.

Chapter Two

Bianca absently rubbed the right side of her bottom as she made her way through the maze of tables towards the one where a man sat alone, a bottle of wine his only company.

He watched her approach with an unwavering gaze, and for the second time that day Bee felt self-conscious. What did he see? The same as she did when she looked in the mirror? A woman who'd passed her teens years ago, leaving behind her nubile, youthful body? Did he notice the dimples in her thighs? Or the breasts that weren't quite as firm as they'd once been? What about the extra kilos she'd picked up over the last year, using food for comfort—and as a substitute for sex?

God, she missed sex. That was one thing she and Rick had never had trouble with. When they'd hit the sheets, the sheets had more often than not landed on the floor—on top of them. Vigorous, enthusiastic lovemaking had always been their strong point. Whatever else had gone wrong in their marriage, it hadn't been a physical problem. Even now, thinking about Rick's prowess increased Bee's body temperature.

That, combined with the rush of awareness that came from Brody's appreciative glance, made her breasts tighten and her heart thump. Bee took a second to enjoy the sensation. She felt alive. And she hadn't felt that in so very long.

"Are you okay?" Brody enquired as she approached the table.

"Of course I am. Why d'ya ask?"

"Because you have a red splotch on your, uh, butt cheek."

Bee broke into a huge grin. "You're checking out my arse?"

He snorted. "It's hard not to, Ms. Rogers. The way you're rubbing it, every man within a one-mile radius of the pool is checking it out."

"I have to rub it," she said as she took a seat opposite him. "It's sore."

He looked at her in exasperation. "You just said you were okay."

"Well, what did you want me to say? I hurt my butt?"

"Did you?"

"Hurt it? Yeah. But it wasn't my fault. I was attacked."

His exasperation turned to alarm. "Attacked?"

"Attacked," she confirmed. "Here's a word of advice. Never try to convince a bride she'll look good in a photograph with her groom's teeth attached to her thigh. She won't appreciate it."

Brody squeezed his eyes shut and lifted up a finger. "You suggested Aidan bite Mack on the leg? For a photograph?"

"Not bite," Bee corrected. "I simply asked if Kennedy—

the hotel photographer—would take a piccie of Danny removing Mack's garter…with his teeth."

He opened his eyes. "And Mack attacked you for this?"

"She pushed me off the chair." Bee snapped her fingers. "Just like that."

"Did you suggest anything else?"

"I might have said Mack should pin a sign on the back of her wedding dress saying 'It took me long enough.'"

"You might have?"

"Okay. I did."

He tipped the bottle over the edge of her glass, pouring her a healthy serving of wine. "And how did Mack respond to that one?"

Bee had the grace to blush as she mumbled her answer.

"Pardon?" Brody poured some wine for himself.

Bianca cleared her throat. "She pointed out that she'd at least waited until she was out of nappies before getting married. Unlike some people she knew."

He raised an eyebrow. "Some people?"

"Me. And my husband."

Vey slowly, Brody set the glass he'd been raising to his mouth back on the table. "You're married."

She sighed. "I was married. Not so much anymore."

"And that means…what, exactly?"

Bee stared into her own glass. She so didn't want to go here. So didn't want to have this conversation. "We're separated. Divorcing."

Pain lanced her chest.

Damn it. She thought she'd worked through all of this. Worked through the hurt.

"I'm sorry," Brody whispered.

"Me too," she whispered back, and took a deep sip of

wine, not quite able to meet his eyes.

"For what it's worth," Brody said quietly, "I am too."

"You're what too?"

"In the middle of a divorce."

She raised her gaze to look at him. This time she couldn't deny what she saw in his eyes. Regret. Hurt. Sadness. "It sucks, doesn't it?"

"Big-time," Brody agreed. "So," he said with a deep sigh, "you were young when you got married?"

"Seventeen. He was eighteen." She shrugged. "We got married on the last day of school. All our friends went to Queensland for Schoolies week, you know, to party and celebrate. We went to the Holiday Inn in Newcastle on honeymoon."

Brody regarded her with serious eyes. "Would you rather have gone to Schoolies?"

"God, no." She smiled at him. A secret smile, filled with memories of days and nights spent in bed, naked. "Our honeymoon was the best weekend of my life."

He smiled back, telling her he understood every one of those memories. "Mine too."

She wrinkled her nose. "It's a funny thing. How life goes on and honeymoons get left in the past and marriages end."

"Funny strange, or funny ha-ha?"

"Funny strange. There's nothing funny ha-ha about it."

"But it was the right decision for you? Splitting up?"

"It was the only decision." She bit her lip. "That's quite an, uh, intimate question."

He gave her an apologetic look. "I'm sorry. It's probably none of my business. It's just that…" His voice trailed off.

"It's just what?" In that instant, he looked so desolate, so alone, Bee wanted to cross the table, take him in her arms and hold him until his pain lessened. Until her hurt ebbed slowly away.

Or perhaps Bee was just looking for a reason to touch him. Hadn't she been thinking about it constantly, the entire way through the meeting with the photographer? How much she'd like to wrap her arms around Brody? Feel his arms around her? How their brief encounter earlier had left her hungry to get to know him better? Physically and emotionally?

"It's something I've been questioning a lot lately," Brody said. "Whether separating was the right decision. I keep asking myself if there wasn't something else we could have done to make it work. Something I could have done."

God, she could so understand. The same questions had haunted her for months. "And was there? Something you could have done?"

Brody wiped his hand over his mouth and chin. The light shadow of a beard rasped against his skin. At a guess, she'd say he hadn't shaved this morning. "Maybe. Probably. Or maybe not." He sighed. "At the time it seemed like the right thing to do."

Bee cleared her throat. "Well, this conversation got a lot more intense than I'd anticipated."

"It did, didn't it?" He looked surprised. "Tell you what. Let's not talk about divorce for the rest of lunch. We can discuss anything but. Deal?"

Bianca nodded her approval. "Deal."

Brody signaled to a waiter. "You okay for me to go ahead and order a couple of grilled cheese sandwiches? Or would you prefer something else?"

"Grilled cheese would be perfect."

"On brown bread?"

Bianca shook her head. "Turkish."

He raised an eyebrow. "I had you pegged as a brown bread person."

She smiled. "I used to be. But my tastes have changed."

"That seems to happen to all of us as we get older, doesn't it?"

Bee shrugged. "I guess it's part of maturing. You learn things about yourself you never knew when you were younger."

"I can relate to that." Before Brody could elaborate, the waiter approached, and Brody ordered for both of them, checking with Bianca that he had everything correct.

Bee appreciated both the fact that he took charge and that he didn't assume anything about her. She appreciated a lot about him, she realized, starting with the physical and moving right along to his behavior and honesty.

"So tell me, Mr. Evans, what you do when you're not escaping real life in a tropical paradise," Bianca said as the waiter walked away with their order.

"I run an auto repair shop in Newcastle."

"Newcastle? I live there too. Talk about coincidence."

He grinned. "Oh, yeah. A real coincidence."

"So, an auto-repair shop? As in, you fix broken cars?"

"I do."

"Like a mechanic?"

"Nope. Like a panel beater. We deal with body repairs."

She dropped her gaze to his hands and then couldn't resist following her gaze with her own hand. She stroked her fingers over his. A quick stroke, nothing too intimate or personal, just a precursor to what she said next. Well, that was what she told herself anyway. Especially when the feel of his fingers made her belly flutter.

"So you work with damaged cars on a daily basis, yet your hands are spotless. I'd at least expect to see grime under your fingernails."

"There's this amazing invention," he told her, straight-faced. "Keeps the hands and nails spotless. It's called... soap."

"Soap?" She looked at him with wide eyes. "Really? How does it work?"

"You rub it into your hands with a bit of water, and bam, all that grime comes off. It's amazing."

She gave a dainty snort. "Maybe I should try it someday."

"Maybe you should." He looked sheepish. "I have a confession."

She raised an eyebrow.

"Soap isn't the real reason my hands are clean. I, er, I don't actually do the repairs myself. Not anymore."

"You don't?"

He shook his head. "Nope. I've kind of extended the business in the last year. Added a whole other shop."

And just like that, Bianca found herself fascinated. "A shop that doesn't require getting your hands dirty?"

"Uh-huh. I've opened up a spare parts business too. "

"In the same place?"

"Next door. The space came up for lease, and the second I saw the sign, I knew it was time to expand. Now, if you ever need a new part for your car, you can come to me." He beamed at her.

"I'll keep that in mind." She'd never had to deal with car troubles before. Rick had always taken care of things for her. "How's the new business going?"

"Picking up every day."

"And the old? If you're working in the new shop, is that

suffering at all?"

A shake of his head this time. "I put my floor manger in charge of repairs. He was up for a promotion anyway, and he's good at his job. So far, it's all working out well."

Bianca regarded him with interest. "Sounds like it could have been a lot to take on. Especially at a time when you're going through emotional and personal upheaval." Sheesh, could she sound more like a social worker? Bee mentally shook herself. Yeah, the whole prospect of "dating" again was new to her. Didn't mean she had to slip into her professional persona to deal with it. She was an adult now. She could handle life on a personal level.

Brody's ocean-colored gaze trapped hers, making her breath catch.

"It was a good time to take on a new project. I'd become bored with the repairs. I'd had enough. Had even begun hating my work." He grimaced. "I used to dread getting up in the morning."

Bianca's heart clenched. "You did?"

Brody inhaled. "Never spoke about it much, but yeah. Hated work. The new business has given me a new lease on life. It keeps my mind off my personal troubles and my brain stimulated at work."

The waiter returned with their food, and as Brody tucked in, Bianca spoke, picking up the conversation as if there hadn't been an interruption. "I can relate to that."

Brody looked at her questioningly. "You also hated your work?"

"No. I love my work. Always have." Bianca was a medical social worker. She'd studied hard for the qualification, relying on Rick to support her while she got her degree. He'd never once complained about having to work hard to put her through uni. He'd done nothing but encourage her.

Funny, she'd kind of forgotten that in the last few years. It took chatting with Brody to jog the memories out of her subconscious. "I mean, I also took on a new project after my marriage broke down." She bit into her toasted cheese. As different as it tasted from the one she and Rick had eaten on their honeymoon, memories from that evening still filled her head. She shoved them neatly aside.

Brody didn't respond. He simply waited for her to swallow and continue speaking.

"I started doing some voluntary work at the fire department."

Brody blanched. "You're a fiery?"

"God, no," she was quick to reassure him. "I'm way too scared to ever put myself in the line of fire like that. Er, so to speak."

He grinned and took a healthy swallow of wine. Bianca did too.

"No, as a social worker I run support groups there twice a week. One group is for victims of fires and the other for fieries who've experienced trauma while on the job."

"Sounds intense."

"It is. But it's something I'd wanted to do for a while now."

He looked surprised. "It is?"

"Yeah." She ate a bit more toasted cheese, remembered the shared laughter and the rapturous moans of her honeymoon and forced herself to focus on the present, not the past. "See, last year, after Danny was trapped in a fire while on the job, well, I got majorly freaked out. Suddenly the possibility of him or my father dying or being seriously injured became very, very real." Both her brother and father worked as firemen. It was kind of a genetic thing with the men in her family. There wasn't a generation gone by that didn't have a Rogers fiery in its midst.

"I needed to do something useful for a change. Help out at the station, I guess. And since I'm way too much of a coward to ever work in the field, I figured I'd put my skills to use as best I could. Besides, I found I suddenly had a lot of spare time on my hands." Her evenings had grown very quiet and very lonely without Rick. And since they hadn't had any children, Bianca was well and truly alone.

Pain stabbed her heart, but she pushed it aside and concentrated on Brody.

He regarded her with intense eyes for the longest time. "I'm impressed," he finally said. "Very impressed. Must take it out of you though." He bit into his sandwich.

Heat slammed into Bianca. Dear Lord, even with his mouth full, the man was sexy. She almost offered him a bite of her sandwich—so she could have a close-up of his lips closing around the food. She and Rick had shared their grilled cheese. Couldn't she and Brody?

"Sometimes it does. Sometimes it's hard to keep my distance and I get too involved, especially if I know one of the fieries in the group." She shrugged. "But I've been a social worker for a long time. I've learned how to keep my distance." She'd learned how to keep her distance from Rick as well. Just another part of their whole big suitcase of problems.

"Are you happy with the volunteer work?"

"I am." She smiled then. "It's been a tough year to be happy, but this definitely helps. Are you happy with your shop?"

He smiled too. "Yep. I really am. It's nice to be stimulated again. To do something that excites me."

It was on the tip of her tongue to ask if he'd found a woman that excited him since the breakdown of his marriage, but she figured that question held way too many landmines. She studiously avoided it.

And then the devil came out to play, and although she considered sending it back into hiding, Bianca decided to let it stay. She let a small smile play on her lips. "I know of something else that might stimulate and excite you."

Brody sat up in his chair. "You do?" His eyes glinted, and the heat that had slammed into her earlier spread fast.

"Yeah, I do." She winked. "Finish up, and then it'll be my pleasure to show you."

Chapter Three

"A pool?" He looked from her to the water and back again in disbelief. "This is your idea of exciting and stimulating?"

She grinned at him. "A cool dip on a hot day. Stimulating, for sure."

He held up his hands in defeat and gave a soft snort. "Okay. I'll admit it. You got me good with that one. A swim was the last thing on my mind."

She gazed at him with wide-eyed innocence. "You thought I was referring to something else?"

He didn't gaze back, exactly. No, she'd never describe the smoldering, sensual look he shot her as a gaze. Devastating, perhaps. A jumpstart to her libido, maybe, but not a gaze.

"Not thought. Hoped."

"Brody…" Without realizing it, she'd placed her hand on his chest. Suddenly her palm was smoking, burning against his firm pecs and smooth skin.

Sheesh, what was it with her and touching him? She couldn't seem to help herself. But then his chest did feel incredible beneath her palm. Hot. Strong. Appealing.

So very, very appealing.

"Yeah?" He placed his hand over hers, holding it close to that warm, strong and appealing chest of his. His heart beat a steady rhythm beneath her hand, reminding her again of how alive she'd felt since barreling into him.

Bianca shook her head. "I have no idea what I wanted to say." His eyes were so blue and so green and so beautiful, she found herself getting lost in them.

The air between them crackled. Well, not really, but it sure felt like it did to Bianca. Felt as if something electric zipped between them, from his chest into her hand. An awareness, a connection.

She liked the feeling. It heated her blood. Made her breasts perk up with interest and her belly flutter with anticipation.

It was Brody who broke the connection, but only to let his gaze wander away from her eyes, down past her neck and breasts...although it settled there for a few brief seconds before continuing on.

He might as well have run his hands over her skin, the way his gaze burned wherever it landed. It gave her both goose bumps and shivers at the same time, and she knew he'd see the telltale signs of her arousal in the millions of fine hairs standing to attention all the way down her arms.

What would he make of them?

His gaze landed on her left hip, and he did a double-take. "You have a tattoo?"

Bianca's hand found it an instant after his gaze did. She yanked her fingers from his chest and traced them lightly over the stem of the tiny red rose, lying below the strap of her bikini bottom.

"I do."

She'd had it done a few months back, after she'd been living alone for a while. She'd wanted to do something crazy, impulsive. Something to show her life was changing, show she was moving on. She'd gone and done the last thing she'd ever have thought she'd do, the last thing Rick would ever have thought she'd do. "It's new. I'm still not used to having it."

Brody kept staring. "Is that a…bee on the petals?"

She smiled. "It is." Her symbolic bee, with its wings spread while it stood steadily on the rose. Free to fly, yet happy to have found its feet in a safe place. "I was never into tattoos before, and the idea of getting one always scared the bejeepers out of me, but now that it's there, well, I kinda like it." She stroked the petals.

Brody's face filled with appreciation. "I kinda like it too."

"You do?" His expression made her mouth water.

He nodded. "It's sexy." His voice dropped about six tones. "Bloody sexy." When he looked back into her eyes, his were the color of a polished aquamarine. They took her breath away. Or maybe the way he looked at her did. As though he'd like to get to know her tattoo a little better. A whole lot better. Quite intimately, in fact.

She couldn't help it. She pictured him on his knees, his face by her hip, his mouth nuzzling the rose, tracing the outline of every petal.

"Brody." His name was a whisper.

"Did it hurt?"

"What?"

"The tat. The needle."

"A little." More than that. But pain was not topmost on

her mind right now. Desire was. Her belly was a swirling mass of lust. Wet heat pooled between her legs. More than anything she wanted Brody's tongue on her hip. Wanted to feel the scrape of his beard against her bare skin as he explored the bee.

"I would have kissed it better." Now his voice was a whisper.

"You still could."

"It still hurts?"

"Oh, yeah," she lied. "Heaps."

He reached out, brushing his fingers over the tattoo, over her fingers. "I'd kiss it here." He traced the lone leaf on the stem. "And here." She almost shuddered in ecstasy as he drew his finger along the tiny stem. "And perhaps I'd lick it…here." He stopped at the part were petals met stem.

"Y-you'd have to concentrate real hard. The rose is small. You m-might miss the spot."

"I'd give it my full attention. I promise." He stepped closer, caressed the bee and rose from top to bottom. And maybe caressed a little bit of her hip as well.

"It would…" She cleared her throat. "It would require your full attention."

Desire, red-hot and lightning-quick flooded her body. It swept her away on a tide of passion, clouding her thoughts, fogging her brain. Brody stood so close his scent drifted through her nose, his aftershave sinfully seductive: mellow notes of the outdoors and subtle suggestions of man and musk. If she could bottle his scent she would. She'd keep it beside her bed to sniff at night. And in the morning. And perhaps once or twice during the day, as well.

Then she heard it. The booming, familiar laughter. The unmistakable sound of a man's mirth, followed by a higher-pitched feminine chuckle.

Panic hit her full in the chest.

Oh, shit. She wasn't prepared for this. Wasn't sure how to deal with the situation.

She should run. Fast. Turn and head for her room. Or the sea. Or the safety of the forest behind the hotel. Anything to get away. Otherwise she'd have to deal with something she wasn't at all ready to deal with. But running wasn't an option. It would draw attention to her.

Bee sprang into action. She did the only thing she could think of on the spur of the moment. Bracing herself, she shoved Brody with all her might.

No small feat, taking into account her size and his stature. He weighed at least double what she did. But she had both the element of surprise on her side and a sudden, desperate need for privacy. Coupled with a hit of adrenaline, they gave her the strength she needed.

The unsuspecting Brody lost his footing and tumbled backward into the pool.

Problem was, Bianca pushed him with such force, she couldn't stop the momentum once Brody's body no longer counterbalanced hers. She hit the water maybe a second after he did. And then stayed under a couple of seconds longer than her screaming lungs allowed, knowing he was going to be hopping mad when she surfaced.

Well, that was if he'd hung around long enough for her to surface. After all, what man in his right mind would stick around after that stunt?

She popped her eyes and nose out the water, deliberately keeping the rest of her face hidden.

Brody *was* still there — gaping at her. Looking at her as if she'd lost her mind. Then his jaw firmed, his eyes filled with determination, and as much as Bianca wanted to stay hidden beneath the surface, she no longer had a choice.

Brody closed the space between them, placed a hand on either side of her waist and hauled her upwards until she hung there, suspended, her legs in the water, the rest of her body out of it, her nose in line with his.

Water cascaded from his hair over his shoulders and his eyes blazed. "You have two seconds to explain your actions, Ms. Rogers. Two. Seconds."

"No." She kicked out desperately, then instantly regretted it, fearing the splash would bring attention to them. "No, wait, you don't understand—"

"One..."

"Please. Shh," she begged. "You have to be quiet."

"Quiet?" he snapped. "Are you out of your mind?" He sure looked at her as if she was.

"Um, maybe. Okay, yes, probably. But for now can you please shut up and not say another word and not move even one inch. Please?" She dared to glance behind him, up to the area she'd heard the laughter coming from, and her very worst fears were confirmed. "Shit," she muttered, and ducked her head down, grateful once again for the lovely expanse of Brody's chest. At least this way she was hidden from view.

"Bianca." Brody's voice was stern, and she knew she had to distract him quickly.

"Okay, tell you what. Making as little noise as possible, put me down and walk with me over to the other side of the pool. Way on over to the other side. As far from the bistro as you can get. I'll explain everything then."

"Is there someone standing behind us you don't want to see?" Brody asked, understanding finally settling in those beautiful eyes.

"Two someones, actually. And if there are two of them, I can only assume there are gonna be a lot more any minute. So can you please move? Quickly and quietly?"

Brody raised an eyebrow. He made no effort to release her. "If I put you down and we both walk across the pool, there's going to be a lot more splashing and movement than if only one of us walks."

Bee stiffened. Brody's logic made sense, but she had a particular aversion to being carried. It had a lot to do with Rick's tendency to pick her up whenever he'd thought she needed his help.

Her indecision must have played out on her face, because Brody lowered her into the water.

"No, wait." Her choice was made in a split second. Brody was right. The more they moved, the more likely they were to be noticed. "Don't let me go," she said quietly.

With a small nod, he shifted her back up and began to wade through the water across the pool.

"Thank you," she whispered, not daring to look over his shoulder again.

"At least move a little closer," he growled softly. "Wrap your legs around my waist so I don't feel like I'm walking against you and the water."

Bianca complied immediately, keeping her actions as effortless as possible. No more splashes from her. No more wild kicks.

"Good," Brody muttered. "Now put your arms around my neck so I can use my arms to propel us forward."

By the time Bianca had done as he'd asked, Brody was walking far more smoothly across the shallow end of the pool. And Bianca's heart beat overtime.

Oh God, he felt good. So damn good. His cool, wet skin pressed against hers, her breasts squashed against his hard chest. She knew she shouldn't be holding him so tight, but somehow she couldn't convince herself to let go. Not even a little bit.

She burrowed her face into his neck, tucking her head under his chin. No way was she letting anyone catch a glimpse of her. Besides, like this, up close, she could get a really good whiff of that scent she wanted to bottle.

Now it was all mingled with chlorine, but damn if it didn't make him smell all the more appealing.

And damn if her nipples weren't tight, aching beads, poking at the wet Lycra of her bikini top. It was all she could do to prevent a soft groan from escaping her throat.

Brody followed the curve of the pool to an area gloriously protected by a huge palm tree surrounded by a clump of ferns and thus hidden from view of anyone standing at the Seaspray Bistro.

The pool must have dipped into the deep end, because water suddenly rushed over her shoulders, and Brody's arm wrapped around her waist, keeping her buoyant.

Seconds later, the arm was gone.

Bee found her back pressed against the wall. A hand appeared on either side of her, telling her the water was too deep for Brody to stand, and he held himself above the surface by clutching the side.

She pulled her face up to look at him and lost her breath because his mouth was that close to hers.

"Two seconds to explain," he demanded. "And don't tell me to shut up now, we're nowhere near whoever it was you didn't want to see."

"My parents," she said on a huff of air. "They were

behind us. Meters away."

Brody's eyes widened.

"I, uh, I didn't want them to see us together."

"Why not?"

"Because, damn it, I'm not ready for anyone to see me with you. Least of all my family. Do you have any idea how many questions they'd have had if they'd found us together, your hand on my hip? Do you have any idea what they would have said?"

A smirk touched his lips, making that lower lip of his so damn sexy, a wave of desire almost knocked Bianca sideways. Even the pool water couldn't keep her cool.

"I think I could imagine." He chuckled.

"I'm sorry I pushed you into the pool. I was desperate." She bit her lip as she watched his face for a reaction.

"I'm not."

"Desperate?"

"Sorry."

"You're not?"

"Nope." He shook his head, and droplets of water hit her skin. "If you hadn't, you wouldn't be all wrapped around me now, and I wouldn't be able to do this." His eyes glittered.

"Do what?" Oh, God. There went her breath again. She couldn't seem to keep it in her lungs when she was around him.

"This." He dipped his head and kissed her.

The soft groan she'd held in earlier escaped. How could she not groan when his lips clung to hers, making fireworks explode behind her eyelids?

He tasted…delicious. Sweet and spicy. So familiar and yet so mysterious. More, she wanted more of him, of his taste. Of his lower lip.

She couldn't resist. Couldn't stop herself. She nibbled on that luscious lip, determined to satisfy her craving to sample it. Only it didn't satisfy. Not even close. It set off a chain reaction inside her, demanding she sample every part of his mouth. His lower lip, his upper one, his tongue…

She parted her lips, seeking to intensify the kiss, and whimpered as his tongue found hers, sliding across it with velvet heat and deadly precision. The erotic caress echoed deep inside her belly. And lower. Much lower.

Bee tightened her hold on him, bracing her arms around his neck and squeezing his waist with her legs, hauling him in closer. The need to feel his skin against hers—all that firm muscle squashed against her chest and her stomach—made her reckless.

So what if they floated in a pool in the middle of the resort? The greenery offered a touch of privacy, and she was in Brody's arms.

He pressed up against her, hard. This wasn't a case of one-sided lust on her part. Brody wanted her as much as she wanted him. The bunched muscles in his shoulders, his labored breath and his stunning kiss were all sure signs.

She silently cursed her height. She lacked the length to mold her groin to his. Wrapped around him like this, her pussy was pressed against his belly, not his cock. She wanted his cock. Wanted to grind herself against its hard length, tease them both with the promise of what could be if neither wore swimsuits. Wanted to confirm he was as aroused, as aware as she was.

She squirmed against him, struggled to lower her waist and yet still kiss him. She never wanted to stop kissing him. Ever. Never wanted to lose his unique taste. Or be deprived of the eroticism of his tongue. The hot, teasing skill of his mouth.

Never mind bottling his scent and keeping it beside her bed, she considered tying him to her bed, keeping him there so she could sniff him at night. And in the morning. And perhaps once or twice during the day as well.

Brody broke the kiss with an agonized groan. "Christ, Bee, you gotta stop."

Bianca froze. "S-stop what?"

"Driving me crazy. Rubbing against me like that." He gritted his teeth as though he were in pain.

"You...don't like it?" Was that her heart climbing into her throat? Was that why she suddenly couldn't talk? Couldn't breathe?

"No," he growled. "I fucking love it. But it's driving me wild. Making me wanna do bad things to you, right here, in the pool—"

"Do them," she demanded. "Right here, in the pool." She twisted her hips this way then that, rubbing herself on his belly, grinding her clit against all that smooth muscle.

Brody squeezed his eyes shut. "Christ, you're a little hellfire."

"Horny hellfire," Bee corrected and molded her mouth to his again.

He wrapped an arm around Bianca, slamming her against his body, holding her so tight she couldn't have possibly escaped—even if she'd wanted to. Which she didn't. Uh-uh. She could happily spend the rest of the afternoon wrapped in this man's arms, cocooned in the tropical waters of the pool, concealed from her parents' view.

Or maybe she couldn't. Because the truth was, they were in a very public pool, and anyone could swim past them at any time. Regardless of how horny she was—and dear

Lord, she was horny—they couldn't do this here. Not if they wanted to do everything Bianca fantasized about.

It astounded her how many fantasies could cram themselves into her head over the period of a couple of minutes, but Bee was pretty sure she'd covered all of them. Whatever a man and a woman could do together, she'd pictured it—and then some.

Perhaps if her entire extended family weren't all currently on the island, she'd have played this scene through to its natural conclusion. But they were there. Every last one of them. And all she needed was for Great Aunty Alberta, or worse, Bee's big brother, to bustle past while she—or Brody—gloried in the throes of a massive orgasm.

If Brody kept on with his sensual assault, if he continued to kiss her like she was the sexiest woman in the world, it wouldn't matter who walked past. She'd simply strip both Brody and herself, and fuck him right there, against the pool wall.

Brody must have sensed her partial reluctance, because he eased his hold on her and brought the kiss down from a roaring inferno to a gentle flame. Which was almost okay with Bianca, because it gave her the opportunity to nibble on his lower lip again.

"You know, I'd have no problem making love to you right here," he murmured when she finally released his luscious flesh, and he loosened his hold on her ever so slightly.

Without removing her arms from his neck, she slipped her legs from his waist and let them slide down the front of his body. At last, she found the evidence of his desire she'd so frantically sought moments ago.

It pressed against her thigh, a solid bulge, thick and long, and so enticing it was all Bee could do to keep her hands around his neck and not draw them down to cover his erection.

"Me either," she sighed, and rubbed her leg against his cock, loving the feel of him, loving his arousal, loving that he was as horny as she was. "But Great Aunty Alberta would have a fit if she saw us."

Brody made a funny sound, as though someone was choking him. "Let's ensure she doesn't. Wanna sneak out the pool and make a mad dash for my room?"

"God, yes."

Before the words were out of her mouth, Bianca found herself being lifted again. One second she was in the water, covered from shoulder to toe in sun-warmed liquid, the next she sat on the edge of the pool. Brody hauled himself out next to her, took her hand and pulled her to her feet. Then he set off in the direction of the lush resort gardens, tugging her along with him.

Chapter Four

"I have a beachside bungalow, not far from where we met this morning," Brody told her as he quickened his pace.

She needed no encouragement to match his steps, although she had to take two for every one of his. "Me too." Excitement fizzed inside her. "Whichever one we get to first, we go into."

"Deal."

Dripping wet, they scooted through the gardens, their steps increasing in speed from a brisk walk to a gentle trot to an all-out run. Bianca was about to shift into sprint mode when Brody took a sudden left and nipped behind an oasis of trees. He took her with him.

"What the…? What are you doing?"

He pressed his finger to her lips. "Shh."

That was when she heard it. Footsteps and animated chatter. She couldn't identify the voices, there were too many of them, but the words *wedding*, *groom* and *bachelor party* drifted her way, and she was suddenly jolly appreciative of

Brody's quick thinking.

Just like she wasn't ready to face her parents, Danny or Great Aunt Alberta, so she wasn't ready for anyone she knew to see her with Brody. Wasn't ready for the speculative glances or raised eyebrows. Wasn't ready for Rick's name to come up while she was with him.

"Good thinking," she whispered.

"Selfish thinking," he whispered back, and kissed her again.

And just like that, Bianca forgot all about the people walking by. Hidden from view, she forgot all about everything except the man who crushed her to him. The man whose back was bent so he could reach her mouth with his. The man whose erection seemed to have grown in the time it took them to cross the hundred meters from the pool to here.

And she knew it had grown because she could feel it. Her hand was on the front of his boardies, cupping him. She had no memory of placing her hand there, just a vague recollection of needing to touch him so badly, she thought for sure she'd die if she didn't.

Brody growled into her mouth but did not release her lips. Which suited her fine, because she wouldn't have let him go had he tried. Not when his tongue did deliciously naughty things to the inside of her mouth. Not when his lips pressed so enticingly against hers. Not when she inhaled the air he breathed.

Brody's soft growl changed to a ragged groan when the barrier of his wet boardies proved too annoying, and she slipped her hand beneath the sodden material, taking his hot, pulsing cock in her palm.

Then it wasn't just Brody groaning. Bianca let out a soft moan, the feel of his hard flesh enough to set fire to her loins.

Satin-covered steel.

She wrapped her hand around him, stroking up and down. Not easy. Not within the confines of his shorts, but God help her, she wasn't letting go. Not for anything. Not when her actions made him shiver as they kissed.

Not when liquid heat filled her pussy, her stomach clenched with desire and her heart pounded fiercely beneath her breast. Not when the throbbing vein lining his dick made her aware of how alive she felt with him. How her own blood roared in her ears.

Pearls of moisture beaded on the tip of his erection. She stopped breathing. Ran her thumb over the wetness. Moaned.

He tore his lips from hers. "Bee…"

Her name was both a salutation and a plea. His eyes blazed with passion.

Their bungalows suddenly seemed very far away. Unreachable.

Didn't matter. They could make it. If they walked really fast. Okay, sprinted, they could do it. Get there before the passion overwhelmed them.

"Room," she gasped. "We can make it if we hurry."

Brody stared at her with wide eyes.

"Not too far," she muttered, her heart slamming into her ribs. "Not far at all."

"Y-you're serious?"

"Dead serious."

Disbelief filled his gaze.

"We can run," she assured him.

His only response was a hoarse laugh. Hoarse and sexy.

Bee would have replied but she couldn't. Her mouth was otherwise occupied. As she'd presented Brody with her best verbal argument, she'd slid to her knees and yanked at the tie on his waistband, torn at the Velcro and finally gotten his boardies undone. Tempting and hard in her hand, his erection now pulsed before her eyes, its tip sodden.

Bee couldn't wait. No longer wanted to. She didn't care where they stood. Trees surrounded them, their thick, lush foliage hiding them from view. She'd been a teenager the last time she'd done anything this bold, this daring. Last time she'd been giddy on fresh air and the great outdoors and a man she desired.

She felt like that teenager all over again. Reckless. Hot. Free. Ravenous.

She licked the moisture off the head of his cock.

"Ah, fuck, Bee." Brody tried to stop her. Grabbed at her arms, attempted to lift her back up, but she nuzzled her mouth against his belly, licking at the sensitive skin there before once again tasting the precome he produced for her.

Instead of lifting her, Brody ran his hands over her shoulders, caressing, massaging. Logically he might have known they shouldn't do this here. Physically he was in the exact same boat as her—powerless to fight the lust that had sparked between them this morning, flared during lunch and exploded in the pool.

Salt, chlorine and musk flavored her lips. The spongy tip of his cock pressed on her tongue, and Bianca could not restrain herself. She opened her mouth and devoured him. Sucked him deep inside, luxuriating in the sensation of his hard length pulsing between her cheeks.

Her release was slow. A sensual exploration of satiny skin as she pulled off him.

"Bee…honey…" Brody's voice was a low rasp. The vibrations of his words rippled down her spine, making her shiver.

She sucked him back in and then lost track of her actions. She simply enjoyed him, feasting on his succulent flesh, relishing the gasps and muttered curses that filtered through the air above her. She palmed his testicles and stroked the soft skin behind as her mouth made love to him.

Brody began to sway his hips, fucking her lips. No, not fucking. His actions were too gentle for that, too controlled, but Bee followed his lead, hollowing her cheeks, relaxing her tongue, and allowed him to direct his penis in and out of her mouth.

She wrapped an arm around his thighs, let her hand slide over his firm arse cheeks and continued to tease his scrotum.

Brody's fingers tunneled into her hair, tightening and relaxing reflexively, as though he was unaware he moved them in time with his thrusts into her mouth.

Wet heat flooded her pussy. Her breasts ached. Her clit tingled. But most of all, her heart filled. Warmth settled deep inside it, along with a sense of contentment. Of rightness.

The muscles in his thigh quivered. His balls tautened.

Bee would have smiled, but then she couldn't take back control, couldn't increase the suction and bounce her head up and down on his cock.

Brody ceased stroking into her. He grabbed fistfuls of her hair, and his legs stiffened as a groan filled the air.

"Gonna come, Bee. Gonna come so hard, Honeybee."

Emotion welled in her chest. Tears stung her eyes, and her heart skipped a beat.

Honeybee.

He had a nickname for her.

She sucked him in a little deeper this time.

Honeybee. Rick's nickname for her.

Memories crashed over her. Memories of sucking Rick, of what he liked, of his reactions.

She pulled off him, and then took only his tip in her mouth, swirling her tongue around, applying muted pressure as she suckled. Not too much pressure—he'd be too sensitive.

The breath exploded from Brody's mouth. He ceased moving, ceased talking. Tension turned his arse cheeks to rock. His testicles pulled tight in her hand. A soft keening sound filled the air.

Bee released his arse and wrapped her free hand around his shaft, pumping him.

The keening sound increased. He tugged hard at her hair, and then he was coming. Spilling his release in her mouth, pumping over and over again.

Bee swallowed once, and he jerked violently but continued to come.

Long seconds passed before his orgasm faded and his body relaxed, the tension seeping out of it. With a final shudder, one last spurt of semen landed on her tongue, and then he was pulling at her hair, gently coercing her mouth off him. He collapsed to his knees before her, his breath uneven, his cheeks flushed.

She swallowed as he watched her, the blue-green of his eyes almost invisible around his huge pupils.

"Christ…Honeybee." He shook his head as though incapable of further speech. But then, speech was not necessary. Not when he cupped her face, pulled it in close to his and kissed her so thoroughly Bianca shook from head to toe when he was done.

By the time their mouths parted, Bianca was a shaky mess.

Her hands trembled, her lips were swollen and her lungs

couldn't quite find an even pattern of inhaling and exhaling. Her bikini top stretched tight around her aching breasts, and her bikini bottoms were now not only wet from the pool but from the cream that slickened her pussy.

If kissing him had turned her on, blowing him had turned her into a wanton beast. She could think of nothing but fucking him. Lowering herself onto that delicious cock and riding him until pleasure swamped them both.

"That look in your eyes…" Brody's voice was rough, hoarse. "Jesus, it's making me hard again."

Had her mind been on anything other than the complete and utter need to make love to the man, she might have scoffed at his nonsense.

Of course he wasn't hard again. No one could get hard that fast. Not after an orgasm like the one he'd just had. But fire lit his eyes, and a muscle ticked in his cheek, and he looked so damn sexy, Bianca could think only of his growing erection and what it might translate into.

Brody growled. "There is no way I'm taking you here, Bee. No way on earth. You deserve satin sheets and rose petals. Complete luxury and nothing less." He shook his head. "I'm taking you back to my room." He ran his thumb over her lips, dipped it into her mouth, and she licked at it lightly, making him shudder again. "I'm going to lower you onto those sheets and strip you slowly. Leisurely. Then I'm going to take my sweet time making love to you. Tasting every inch of your body. From your mouth to your toes and all those sexy bits in between." He swallowed. "All of them."

"Wh-what if I don't want to wait 'til we get back to your room?" she rasped. No way she'd have the patience to get back there. "What if I want you to do all of those things to me right here?"

He quirked an eyebrow. "And risk sharing you with the mozzies? Not a chance."

As though one had been hanging around waiting for a good opportunity, a mosquito buzzed around her head and landed on her arm. Brody brushed it away.

"My room?" His smile screamed *I told you so*.

"Your room. As quickly as we can get there."

Brody was on his feet in a second, and so was she. He pulled his boardies back into place, fastened them, and before Bee could take a step in any direction, he tossed an arm around her shoulders, leant down, placed another around the back of her legs and swung her up into the air.

Stunned, Bianca had no chance to object as he tucked her against his chest and walked briskly through the clump of trees and back onto the garden path, now free of other wedding guests.

She tried to relax against him. Attempted to enjoy the ride. Tried to appreciate the strength in his arms and the firmness of his lovely chest. She focused on her body, on the heat between her legs and the ache in her breasts.

But with every step the heat cooled and the ache lessened.

God help her, she wanted to stay in the moment. Wanted him to race them back to his room so they could make love. Indulge. Fuck.

Or she had wanted that. Mere seconds ago. Before Brody had hauled her into his arms. Before he'd scooped her up as though she were weightless.

Now, no matter how hard she tried, she couldn't relax. Couldn't retrieve the moment. Not while Brody carried her.

"I can't wait to get you inside, strip you naked, and fu—have my wicked way with you." His voice was rough, his steps unwavering.

She wanted to agree, wanted to writhe in anticipation of what was to come. But she couldn't. Bianca was trapped.

Trapped in Brody's arms.

Trapped in the past. Trapped in Rick's arms, being carried once again.

Her muscles tensed.

Trapped.

Oxygen eluded her. She couldn't breathe.

Instinctively, she struggled against Brody.

He stilled. "Are you okay?"

Yes, she tried to tell herself. She was fine. Everything was fine. And it would be even more fine if they got to his room and he let her stand on her own two legs.

But if that was true, why did claustrophobia claw at her throat? Why did she suddenly feel as if she no longer existed here, in the present, on this magical, tropical island?

Why could she not shake the fear that she'd been thrown back in time and landed slap bang in the middle of her marital problems?

"Bianca?" Concern blazed from Brody's eyes.

She struggled again to free herself. "You…you need to put me down. Please."

Brody didn't hesitate. He set her on her feet.

Disappointment streaked across his face. And confusion. "You're having second thoughts." It wasn't a question.

She stepped back, took a few gulps of air, filled her lungs. "Not second thoughts."

"Then what?"

Oh, God. How to explain?

She captured the first word that came to mind. "Flashbacks."

"Flashbacks?"

"I…" No, not her. "My husband…"

Brody's voice deepened. "What about him?"

She took a few more steadying breaths, found her feet planted steadily on the ground. Appreciated it.

"H-he used to lift me up. Like you did."

Brody looked at her intently, waiting for a better explanation. His stance might appear relaxed, but Bee wasn't fooled. There was nothing calm or tranquil about the way he looked at her. He was alert, listening. He was…tense.

"He had a habit of carrying me," she scrambled to clarify.

Regret rushed her. She'd killed the moment. Broken their carnal connection. Brody wasn't about to haul her into his bungalow now, strip her naked and fu—have his wicked way with her.

He was too busy waiting for her explanation. And maybe being wary of her words.

"H-he—Rick—would pick me up whenever he thought I needed help."

At first she'd loved Rick's shows of masculinity. Loved that he was big enough, strong enough to lift her, help her over a puddle, give her a boost up a steep hill, carry her when they were in a hurry, step in front of her if he feared danger of any kind.

Brody blinked. "And that was a problem for you?"

"Not in the beginning." Her hands fluttered at her sides. "I wouldn't have minded so much if it had just been about him carrying me physically." Her stomach rolled as she realized what she was about to do—discuss an issue in her marriage she'd never discussed with Rick. How would Brody take it? "The thing is, he started carrying me emotionally too."

Brody frowned. "I'm not sure I understand."

Why would he?

She clasped her hands together to stop their restless fluttering. "I was immature when we got married. I went from my parents' home, where they looked after me, to my own home with Rick. And I let him do what my parents had done. Look after me, make decisions for me."

Brody cleared his throat. Bianca thought he was going to say something in response, but instead he signaled to a bench a few meters away. "Why don't we sit down for this?"

She nodded. "Good idea."

Brody made no attempt to help her get there. He didn't carry her, he didn't even put a hand on her lower back to steer her, as Rick would have done.

They sat stiffly, side by side, looking across the gardens and over the beach.

"You were saying?" Brody prompted.

Bee stared out at the ocean sparkling in the distance. It was easier looking there than at Brody. "It suited me. I liked being cared for. Liked not being involved in anything more important than deciding what we had for dinner at night."

"So what changed?"

"I did." She waited, let the concept settle in his mind. And hers. "I started to grow up and learn a whole lot about myself I'd never known before." Her social work studies had helped with that. "I began to understand who I was and how I'd just switched my parents for him."

"So you saw him as a father figure?" Brody sounded appalled.

Bee chuckled at the thought. "Hardly. We were far too physically compatible for me to ever mistake him for my father. But I did let him organize my life—until I realized I was as responsible for our relationship and well-being as he was." She sighed deeply. Was it any wonder Rick had said no to children? He already had a child living with him. "Thing is, I twigged too late, because by then Rick was used to his role. He'd even taken it one step further."

"Further how?" Was that reluctance she heard in Brody's voice?

"He'd started carrying all the problems in our lives too. Keeping them quiet so as not to worry me. He stopped talking to me about issues. I never knew if something worried him because he never told me." She sighed deeply, ruing her immaturity, her stupidity.

It had taken her a while to realize their marriage was falling apart, because Rick wouldn't let her see how upset he was by the distance that had grown between them. Right until the end he'd refused to speak openly with her, yet still tried to carry and protect her. And the more he did, the more frustrated she'd become. The more claustrophobic she'd felt. And the more distant they'd grown.

"And you never explained to him how much you needed him to let you...walk on your own two feet." It was more of a statement than a question.

Bee finally turned to look at him. "Only after it was too late." A year too late.

Brody was silent for a long moment. "I'm glad you told me."

She looked at him in surprise. "You are?"

He nodded. "If I'm unaware of what worries you then I can't avoid doing it. This way at least I know. No carrying Bianca. Not physically or emotionally."

She took his hand in hers. "That doesn't mean I don't like being touched. I do. Very much. And...I especially like being touched by you."

A soft breath escaped him, like a sigh of relief. "I'm glad to hear that, since I enjoy touching you. Very much."

"D-do you think we could go back to your room now, so you could touch me again? Maybe all over this time?"

Brody looked at her. "Would it be okay if I held your hand as we walked there?"

She smiled. "It would be very okay."

He waited until she'd stood before getting up himself, and then he let her take the first step before falling in beside her as they walked.

Bianca smiled to herself, noting how his behavior had changed from one extreme to the other. And all because she'd been brave enough to voice her concerns, something she'd never done adequately during her marriage.

They walked slowly. Gone was the urgency of before, until Brody leant down and whispered in her ear. "You know, I still can't wait to get you back to my room and have my wicked way with you."

And then they were running again, sprinting along the path, Bianca chuckling as they went. Her shoulders felt curiously light, and she knew she'd done the right thing setting Brody straight. Now, wherever they were headed, they'd at least go there on equal footing.

Chapter Five

Breathless, Bianca stared at the beachside bungalow. "Your room is right next door to mine."

"How's that for coincidence?" He grinned and yanked her hand. "Mine's still closer than yours. Let's go."

And then they were inside, the door was closed and there were no family members or wedding guests approaching from any angle. It was just Bianca and Brody.

Her heart stuttered. "Uh, I think I should warn you. I haven't done this in a while."

He raised an eyebrow. "Walked into a hotel room?"

"No, stupid. This." She motioned between the two of them. "Sex."

His eyes filled with concern. And with a twinkle. "Think you've forgotten how?"

Bee nodded gravely. "Alas, yes. I have absolutely no memory of what comes next."

Brody hesitated for a second before he answered. "I could show you. Hold your hand through every step—if you'd be okay with that."

She smiled at him. "As long as you don't carry me, that'd be perfectly okay."

He stepped closer. "First thing is to get rid of anything that may interfere with what we're about to do. Which means your bikini needs to go."

"Go where?"

"Away. Off. Somewhere else."

"Ah. Okay. And, er, how would I do that?"

Another step closer. "First, you'd need to pull on this bow here." Brody feathered his hand over her back and tugged on the tie there.

Bee's bikini top slackened immediately.

"And...then?" Her voice came out like a whisper.

"And then we pull on the second bow." His hand threaded beneath her hair, stopped and tugged again. "Right here."

The top slipped off and dropped to the ground.

Bee's breath caught. Her nipples tightened painfully at the sudden freedom. "A-and then?"

But Brody didn't answer. He'd stepped back, and his gaze was focused on her bare chest. A shudder trembled through his shoulders, and with a soft, reverent moan, he raised his hands.

Bianca's eyes slid shut. The rough skin of his palms teased her nipples before he cupped her breasts, holding them as though he was doing nothing but appreciating their weight and texture.

It had been so long since someone had touched her like this. Intimately. She'd missed it. So damn much. Wanted more, wanted his mouth on her breasts, his hands moving, exploring, caressing. She wanted—

Brody gave it to her. His hand disappeared, and his

warm, moist lips closed over a nipple, tugging it into his mouth. The pull wasn't gentle. It was firm, assertive, and Bianca felt it all the way to her bones. Her stomach dipped and swirled. Gooseflesh popped up over her skin, and a long, contented sigh escaped her throat.

Brody plumped her breasts together, held them close and moved over to the other nipple, subjecting it to the same sweet torment: kissing, suckling, nipping, abrading with his teeth and kissing again.

Tears filled Bianca's eyes. It was...beautiful. Sensual. *Intimate.* It made her feel stunning. Wanted. Adored.

She hadn't felt any of that for so long. Had begun to doubt her own sexual appeal since the separation. The lack of Rick's constant assurances had left her floundering.

But Brody brought it all back. The confidence, the security, the knowledge that even though she no longer had the body of a teenager, she was still attractive. His appreciative moans filled the air, and his talented mouth drove her wild.

Liquid fire pooled between her legs, and she arched her back, pressing her breasts harder against his lips, hoping to feel the rasp of his tongue move lower, over her belly and downwards.

When at last Brody raised his head, his eyes were dark blue, all sign of green gone from their depths. "Next...step."

She tried to look at him expectantly, but knew she'd failed when he swallowed hard. "Christ, Bee. Look at me with those bedroom eyes for one more second, and I'll take you right here, on the floor, and the rest of those steps be damned."

Bianca nodded her encouragement. She'd have instructed him to forget the rest of it—*begged* him to—only her voice seemed to have vanished, and in its place was a low groan of anticipation.

"Next step," Brody said with renewed determination. "Remove any remaining clothing that might be deemed obstructive to procedures."

Hah. That one was a no-brainer. Bianca's hands found his boardies, and for the second time that afternoon, she freed him from the pants. Only this time she didn't stop at freeing him. She shoved those swim shorts right down to the floor, leaving Brody wearing absolutely nothing.

He didn't give her the opportunity to appreciate his nudity or his rigid erection. He was too busy sliding her bikini bottoms over her hips, down her legs and insisting she kick them off. Then he knelt at her feet, placed a hand on either side of her waist, leant in and pressed the lightest kiss above the crease between her left leg and hip. Right on top of her tattoo.

"No stinging," he whispered, before tracing his tongue around the rose and bee. So gentle was his caress, Bee almost couldn't feel it. But the butterfly-soft sensations stirred her as much as the strong pull of his mouth on her breasts had. It stirred her to unimaginable levels of lust. A wicked tease that turned her knees to jelly and made her legs shake uncontrollably.

From the minute she'd gotten the tattoo she'd loved it—but never more so than this very second. Never more so than with Brody's mouth sampling every stroke of color. And when that mouth settled into another tender kiss, though she couldn't see, she knew from his position that his lips were centered on the bee. The honeybee.

As he nuzzled her tender skin, his hand made its way up her inner thigh, and with deadly precision, came to settle on her pussy. With his touch way firmer than his kiss, he drew a finger over her inner lips, parting them beneath the pressure. Warm liquid spilled from her core as hot chills raced up her spine.

He didn't pause, didn't hesitate, he slid that finger inside her, burying it as deep as it could go.

Bianca shoved her hand over her mouth to muffle her cry. For the first time in a year, a man had his hand on her pussy. In her pussy. God, it felt so good. So right. So… provocative. Made her want more. A whole lot more. Made her want everything.

He gave her more, sliding a second finger inside her. That in itself would have made her moan, but as he did so, he turned his head slightly, so this time when he kissed her, it was not the tattoo that his lips met. It was her clit. Her aching, swollen clit. The moan became a stifled cry as she pressed her hand harder against her mouth.

"No," Brody said against her tender nub, "don't hide your cries. Don't hide anything from me."

When he swiped his tongue over that tender nub, Bianca didn't try. She dropped her hand to his head, tunneled her fingers into his hair, and with a throaty, unrepressed groan, begged for more.

Brody gave it. He moved his fingers in and out, curving them to her shape, plunging them in at the same speed as he laved her clit. Slow, lazy flicks of his tongue, up-down, up-down.

It was heavenly torture. With every thrust of those fingers, he touched something inside her, something deep, a knot of nerves that increased her pleasure exponentially. But that wasn't all he touched. With every plunge, every lick, he touched her soul. Reached a part of her she'd repressed for so long. A part that needed to feel love, that needed that soul-deep connection with another person. For more than ten years she and Rick had held that connection. But it had been lost, snapped in the devastation of the divorce.

Yet here was Brody, finding the threads, pulling at them, connecting with her on a level that was more than physical. Here was Brody—*Oh, God!* Here was Brody, sliding a third finger inside her. Stretching her. Licking her with fervor, a passion that made her head spin.

Her restraint snapped. Tongues and fingers and soul-deep connections were no longer enough. She wanted one thing, and she wanted it now. Sheets and beds be damned. She had no time for them.

She yanked on Brody's hair, none too gently, and pulled away from him. Before he had time to object, she lowered herself to the floor, straddled his thighs, forcing him to sit back, and took his mouth in an impatient kiss, pressing her body to his.

His erection jammed between their bellies, leaving a damp trail on her skin. Damp—but nothing compared to the moisture that spilled onto his thigh as she ground against him.

She nipped at his tongue, ate at his mouth, demanding he kiss her back, and when he did, when his lips seduced and his mouth devoured, she moaned deep in her throat. His thigh wasn't what she wanted. Not even close.

She squirmed against him, wiggled her hips, raised her bottom and found his cock. A soft sob caught in her throat as she rubbed her clit against it, fiercely, her climax already building.

Brody tore his mouth away from hers with a harsh groan. "Wait!" He panted, hard. "N-not yet."

"Remembered steps," Bee grumbled as she ground against him. "No…need…guide me…anymore."

"Protection," he rasped against her throat. He sucked at it, stopping short of leaving a mark. "Need…condom."

Condom.

The word stopped her short. Sheesh. When last had she used a condom? When last had she needed one?

The idea of needing one now threw her. A year without sex was an eon of drought. The idea of anything interfering with the smooth feel of male flesh inside her doused her desire the tiniest bit.

She inhaled, once, twice. Wrapped her head around the thought of protection. Hated it instantly. So foreign. So unknown. But if it was necessary… "I…I'm on the pill."

For so many years she'd wished she could stop taking the birth control. Now, just this once, she silently thanked her lucky stars she hadn't.

Brody gazed at her with hungry eyes. "Clean?"

She blinked. "Clean." Since Rick was the only man she'd slept with, ever, there was no risk to Brody as far as that went. Still, the conversation sat uncomfortably with her.

"Me too, Honeybee. I swear it. Would never do this if I wasn't." The sincerity shone from his face, and her instinct told her to believe him. He'd connected with her on that soul-deep level. How could she not believe him?

And then conversation stopped as he kissed her again, a kiss as fierce as the one she'd laid on him. Concerns vanished. Fears were vanquished. Nothing had place inside Bianca's head apart from the insatiable longing that pounded through her once again.

This time when she rubbed her clit against this cock, he didn't stop her. Didn't pull away. This time, he thrust up to meet her, increasing the sensation flooding through her, bringing her closer to the brink.

Time and again they rocked together, until her juices coated his shaft and her lust reached epic proportions. No more teasing. No more torment. She wanted all of him.

Her gaze caught his, and in perfect sync they stopped rocking. This time when Bianca raised her hips, Brody pulled back slightly, positioning himself right beneath her. She grasped his cock to hold him steady and lowered herself onto him.

His fingers were nothing compared to his shaft. With every inch she moved, he filled her more. His erection, full, hard and throbbing, pressed inside her, stretching her wide.

Oh, dear God. Yes. Yes, yes, yes.

She'd missed this. Missed it more than she'd ever believed possible. Missed the closeness that came from a man and a woman coupling. Missed the sensations that flooded her pussy as she enveloped him completely. Missed the intensity and the... *Holy crap!* The pleasure.

Jesus, that felt good. So good, so unbelievably good.

She swept her body up in a graceful arc, lifting off Brody before settling back down on him, enveloping him again.

The low, gratified groans that filled the room could be either of theirs. Bianca couldn't tell. She only knew she was right where she wanted to be, doing exactly what she wanted to do.

Her head fell back as Brody grasped her waist, and as she arched up, sliding up and down him, over and over again, he assisted her, moving her body in time with his measured thrusts.

Like a well-choreographed dance, they made love. They rocked together fluidly, like age-old lovers, each anticipating the other's needs seamlessly.

Brody leant in and nuzzled her neck while Bianca wrapped her arms around his shoulders, holding him as she would a cherished lover. Together they soared. And when sensation built to a peak, and Bianca could no longer hold the rhythm of her dance, when her swaying became erratic, insistent, Brody swept a hand from her hip to her belly and swiped his thumb over her clit.

Bianca exploded. Her entire body stiffened save for the erotic pulsing of her pussy walls, which seemed to clench around his cock a million times over. Every clench increased the sensation. His thumb, so precise in its swipes, sent mad thumps of pleasure rocketing through her, and all the while, the rasp of Brody's irregular breath tickled her ear.

When at last she came down from the high, when her orgasm subsided and she could begin to focus properly with her eyes, it was to find Brody's face scrunched in pain. His jaw was rigid, his teeth clenched together and his eyes squeezed shut.

She stroked her hand over his hair and whispered hoarsely, "Your turn."

That was all it took. With his arms wrapped tight around her, he flipped them both over. Bianca found herself lying on her back, her legs wrapped around his waist. Brody lay above her, his cock still snug in her pussy.

No, not snug. He was moving. Fast, slamming into her, pushing deeper inside than he had been, filling her, plunging, faster, faster—until with a loud cry, he stilled. His entire body turned rigid and then relaxed as he pulsed inside her, bathing her pussy in his come.

Bianca gloried in his release. Her inner walls, hypersensitive from her own orgasm, trembled around his cock. Endless seconds passed before Brody finally collapsed atop her, utterly spent.

"Honeybee," he murmured, his voice throaty and sexy as sin. "That was...perfect."

Chapter Six

Brody lay like deadweight on Bianca—and Bianca could not have luxuriated in the feeling more. She loved the familiarity of having a man's body on top of hers. Loved how comfortable she felt with him and how satiated he'd left her. She let her hands play on his back, sliding her fingers over the grooves of his muscles, caressing his damp skin.

Oh, yeah. Brody Evans was all man, and right now there was no other man in the world she wanted lying above her.

"I guess it's true what they say. It's like riding a bicycle."

Brody chuckled. "Lady, I've been on many rides before, and this one was nothing at all like riding a bicycle."

She laughed too. "I mean you never forget."

"I know what you mean." Brody placed a kiss on her nose. "And believe me, I'll never forget this ride."

She smiled at him. "Me either."

"You sore at all?"

Bianca clenched her thighs, checking for any achy spots. "A little tender, maybe, but not sore."

Brody pushed off her immediately, and Bianca objected out loud, hating the weightlessness around her.

"Shh." He eased her legs apart and settled on his knees between them. "You said you were tender. I need to make sure you're all right." And with that, he buried his face between her legs and kissed her. And kissed her and kissed her and kissed her. Until Bianca completely forgot the tenderness and felt only the dizzying climb to satisfaction all over again.

Her climax was softer this time 'round, less potent, but no less exquisite. She came with his tongue on her clit and his hand on her tattoo, blissful ripples undulating through her body.

Tears filled her eyes, and she had to blink rapidly to try to clear them. The blinking didn't help. The moment was too beautiful, the emotions streaming through her too powerful. Whatever she felt for Brody overwhelmed her. The first man she'd made love to in a year!

All at once she missed Rick terribly. The realization descended so quickly, it shook her. How could she have gone almost a year without his touch, without making love to him? How could she go the rest of her life without it?

Rick had been her rock for her entire adult life. And most of her adolescence as well.

"You're crying," Brody whispered.

Bee nodded. "I am."

He shot her a rueful smile. "Was it that awful?"

She smiled back through her tears. "No. It was that good."

"I don't think I've ever reduced a woman to tears before. Not by my tongue, anyway."

"You brought back a lot of memories for me. That's all.

Memories I've tried to suppress for a long time."

He settled back on his haunches and rested his hands on his knees. "Memories of sex?"

She sniffed. "Memories of making love."

"Is that what we did? Made love?"

She held his gaze for a long time, even as a tear dripped off her nose. "That wasn't just sex for me."

His eyes turned more green than blue. "For me either."

Bee wiped her eyes. "I haven't slept with anyone besides my husband. Ever."

Brody watched her intently. He gnawed at his lower lip. "Have you dated anyone else over the past year?"

"A few guys. But none of them really interested me. I went out with them a couple of times but couldn't take it further than that. I guess I wasn't ready for anything intense." She nudged him with her leg. "How about you? You dated anyone since the big split?"

"I have." He nodded slowly but offered no more information.

Bianca's heart began to pound. She knew she didn't have a right to ask, but she asked anyway. "Have you…made love to anyone else?"

His chest heaved. Then he shook his head. "Not really."

Bianca blinked, attempting to still her racing heart. "Not really?"

"I've slept with a few women."

Bianca tried to breathe. She tried to inhale air into her lungs, tried desperately, but couldn't seem to find any. It was like all the oxygen had been sucked out of the room. Off the island even. "A few?"

"Three."

"Oh." It was all she could think of to say. As primly as

she could, she rose first to her knees and then to her feet, searching for her bathing suit. The top was close by and she scrambled to put it on. The bottoms were a little harder to find. She finally located them on the other side of the couch and pulled them up.

Her movements were stilted. It wasn't easy dressing when she couldn't breathe. It was even harder when pain seemed to rain down on her like a million sharp needles. Her chest ached, and her lungs burned. Surely if she found at least one mouthful of air she'd feel better? But no. It just wasn't there.

"Bee?"

She didn't turn around, couldn't face him. "I need to go now."

"Go where?"

"Home." Home? Really? She hadn't had a real home since Rick had moved out. The small place they'd bought when they'd finally been able to afford one had lost any semblance to a home. It had simply become a house. If she'd thought it lacked the noise and laughter of a big family before they'd split, now it closely resembled a mausoleum. "Er, back to my bungalow. I need to get ready for the cocktail party." Not true. The cocktail party wasn't scheduled to begin for another two hours, at least. And the most she needed to do for that was throw on a dress or sarong over her bikini. Well, maybe shower first, as she was pretty sure she smelled of sex.

Sex.

Like Brody had had. With three other woman.

Anguish cut through her, gutting her, leaving her not only gasping for air, but torn apart, wide open and utterly vulnerable.

His hands settled on her shoulders, startling her. She

hadn't heard him stand or walk over.

"You're upset."

"I'm fine." Or she would be, in a thousand years or so.

"I shouldn't have said anything."

"You should have kept it quiet? Protected me from the truth?" She bit off the last word before she said it. *Again.*

He sighed heavily. "If you wish to hear it, I'll never keep the truth from you. But the last thing I want is to hurt you."

Too late. The hurt was there, and it wasn't leaving anytime soon. "I have to go."

"Really?" His hands left her shoulders. "We hit one little bump and you have to walk away?"

"You slept with three other women." Still no damn air. "That's not a bump. It's…it's a deal breaker."

"Bianca…" His voice trailed off, as though he wasn't sure what to say next. "I'm a single man, separated from my wife, on the verge of a divorce. It's not a crime to sleep with other women."

Oh, the words that welled up in her chest, the things she wanted to say, to spit out at him. But she couldn't. Couldn't find the energy to do it. Couldn't find the guts or the strength. So she focused on something else. "Did you think about those other women when you neglected to wear a condom with me?" She spun around to glare at him.

He looked like he'd been slapped. "That's not fair. I would never, ever put your health, your safety, at risk. Never. I said I was clean. I am."

"So what, you wore condoms with them?"

"If you must know, yes. I did."

Bianca threw her hand up in the air, stopping him from saying any more. She didn't want to know. She was loath to hear anything about his sexual exploits, anything at all. She didn't want the details of his sex with anyone else.

"Honeybee—"

"I can't do this anymore." She couldn't. Not for one more second.

"Can't do what?"

"Play this game."

He pursed his lips. Relaxed them, opened them to speak and then didn't.

"I can't do it, Rick." The words came out on a loud sob. "I can't pretend you're not my husband. Can't pretend you're not the man I've loved my whole life. I can't pretend that hearing you've…you've…" The words almost choked her. "You've slept with other women doesn't affect me at all."

His betrayal tangled around her neck and squeezed. Yes, they were in the process of divorcing. Yes, they hadn't been together for a year. But still. This felt so much like Brody… Rick…like *Broderick* had cheated on her, she couldn't bear the hurt or the treachery.

"I…I hadn't expected to see you here." She hiccupped. "Then, when I crashed into you, I thought, maybe we could pretend to be strangers. Pretend we had no history. Wipe the slate clean and start again. I didn't have very high hopes or expectations, I just thought we could try and see where it went." Another hiccup. "But…but it was bloody stupid of me. We aren't strangers. We know each other, and we have a history. We can't pretend it's not there."

"We also can't pretend the last year didn't happen. Can't pretend that we didn't live apart. We're getting divorced, Bianca. I have a ream of documents back in Newcastle stating that fact in black and white. I may have stopped dreaming this year…" Hollow pain filled his voice. "Stopped hoping and stopped wishing, but God help me, I didn't stop living. I still ate and drank and slept and tried to find some kind of facade of a normal life. And if in doing so I had sex, that's not a crime."

"You're right. It's not." Bianca took a deep breath, found the air that had been eluding her and let it fill her lungs. She'd been wrong. Oxygen didn't make her feel any better. It helped her breathe. That was all. The pain still rained down on her, the betrayal tugging even tighter around her neck. "We're over, you and me. You have the freedom and the right to make love to whomever you want to."

"That's just the thing, Bee, it wasn't making love. It was just sex. That's what I recognized—"

She flung her hand up. "I can't. I can't hear this. Can't listen to you speak about sex with another woman. I…I'm not strong enough for that."

"So I can't tell you the stunning realization I came to because of that sex?"

"No. Not interested."

Rick fisted his fingers in his hair, a telltale sign of his frustration. "You just told me I shouldn't protect you from the truth. Not anymore. Now look. You're not giving me a choice. You're forcing me to do the very thing you confessed to hating me doing."

His words slammed into her with such force she had to take a step back to gain her balance.

That's exactly what she'd done. Exactly what she'd always done when Rick had told her something that was too hard to hear. She'd stopped him from saying it, blocked it out.

She floundered, stunned. Walked to the door. Turned back. Gasped and walked back to the door. How could she not have seen that before?

No wonder Rick had stopped telling her anything. No wonder he'd stopped talking so openly to her. She was never strong enough to hear him. Yet this, his confession, this conversation about him fucking some else—three someone elses—was tearing her heart out.

"We just made love, Rick. We just connected again. Connected in a way we haven't connected for in a year. More, damn it. Of course I don't want to hear about your sharing your penis with another woman. It's ripping my insides out. It's breaking my heart all over again."

"If I can't tell you the truth, then what can I tell you?"

"You can tell me the truth. Always. Just not about your antics with other women."

He narrowed his eyes, and she knew she'd given him a mixed message: *Tell me the truth, but only when I want to hear it.* She must have driven him crazy. "Fine. Tell me what you're doing here. Why you're on the island. Why you're staying in the room next door mine. Tell me that." She still reeled from the shock of finding him here. No one had mentioned he'd be attending the wedding. Not Mack or Danny, not her parents, not even Kylie, who'd assigned all the guests their rooms. Surely they'd all known.

"Aidan's getting married. The man who's been as close to me as a brother for ten, more, twelve years is tying the knot. Do you honestly think I'd miss this? You and I may be getting divorced, but he's still my family." His shoulders shook. "I'm losing you, Bee. Do I have to lose *everyone* I love in the process?"

Damn it. How did she argue with him? How did she deny him access to her—and his—family? Danny thought of Rick as his little brother. He had ever since she and Rick had married. She couldn't deny either of them the right for Rick to be at the wedding. She nodded her acceptance warily. "And the room next to mine? How do you explain that?"

He looked at her, trapping her gaze with his, an ocean of agony in his eyes. She couldn't turn away. Couldn't stop staring at the face she knew so well.

"Kylie. I phoned her from Newcastle and asked her to arrange it."

"W-why?"

"Why do you think?"

She shrugged, at a loss.

His face creased in sorrow. "Because I love you. Because divorce isn't what I want. It was never what I wanted. And this year apart, my experiences without you, they've only cemented that fact. I've known since I was seventeen that you were the only girl for me. That hasn't changed. Not ever. Even through the fights and the unhappiness and the discontent and the misunderstandings, I never doubted you were the one. I stare at those fucking divorce papers every night, pen in hand, and I can't do it. I can't sign them. I don't want to sign them. I don't want to lose you. Don't want to lose us. I'm here, in the room next to yours, so we can try to find each other again, so we can remember who we once were together. So we can identify what went wrong and where and change it. I don't want to lose the best damn thing that ever happened to me. You."

Bianca stood rooted to the spot. She couldn't move, couldn't breathe again. He loved her still? Rick loved her?

Her heart expanded, overflowed. His confession stuck in her head. He loved her. Always had. He didn't want the divorce, didn't want them to end.

"I...I love you too." The words came out sounding all

choked up.

He stepped towards her. "Then let's do something about it. Let's make us work again."

"Y-you think that's all it takes? We admit we never stopped loving each other and the problems are gone? Shit, Rick. The issues are still there. All of them." The biggest problem of all haunted her every day. But she couldn't bring it up now. Didn't have the strength to argue her case again. "You've still kept things from me, and I've refused to listen to you. I still do. I can't talk to you—we can't have a decent conversation. I don't know who you are anymore."

He'd hated his work. Hated it so much he'd started another business so he wouldn't have to face going into a job he despised everyday. Why didn't she know that about him? How could she have been so blind to the fact? She'd lived with him, gotten up with him every morning, and they'd gotten ready for their day together. And she hadn't known that every morning he faced his business with a knot of aversion in his stomach.

What about her? She'd never told Rick how much Aidan's accident had affected her or how damn traumatized she'd been that she'd almost lost her brother. How could two people who lived together neglect to speak about vital life issues?

How could their marriage possibly work when their basic communication skills didn't?

"I'm not naïve enough to think the issues are gone." Rick's hand was in his hair again, tugging. "And I'm no longer an idealist. I don't think the problems will be magically resolved if we know we love each other. But damn it, we can work on them, together. Look what happened today. By talking honestly we've already discovered two major issues of contention. I carry the weight of all our problems by not speaking to you about them, and when I do, you won't listen. Imagine if we forced ourselves to sit down, get the truth out and really hear what the other was saying. Imagine what we'd be able to work out then."

"You sound so logical. So…rational." He made perfect sense. And if they worked together, maybe they could untangle some problems. But no matter how many times they discussed the real issue that stood between them — the main reason for their separation — they'd never come to an agreement. And now, to top it all, there was a new setback: today's unwelcome revelation.

Rick had slept with someone else. And as much right and reason as he'd had to do that, Bianca couldn't get past it. She still felt as betrayed, as hurt, as she would have if he'd done it while they were together.

"But?" He dropped his hands. They now curled into tight fists at his sides.

"But now every time I blink, every time my eyes close, all I visualize is you, naked, with another woman. A faceless woman. You — you're making love to her. Fucking her. Fucking *them*. I don't know if I'll ever be able to see you, alone, again. And — " She broke off, heaved in a mouthful of air. "And I don't think…" Fuck, this was hard. So damn hard. "I don't know if…if…I could ever believe it was just you and me in bed again. They…those three…would always be right there with us."

"Bee, please, listen to me. Let me explain. I learned so much about myself and about us, because of them."

"I can't." She shook her head, barely holding it together. "I just can't. N-not now. I'm about to fall apart, and I can't be near you when that happens." Yes, she refused to hear him again, but she was already way too vulnerable, had already revealed way too much of herself to her almost ex-husband. She wasn't physically strong enough to reveal any further weakness. And she didn't think she could bear to hear him, yet again, deny her the one thing she'd wanted so desperately for so many years. "M-maybe tomorrow. Or the next day I'll be ready to listen." She walked backwards, headed for the door. "J-just not now."

And then her hand was on the handle, and she was running outside, breathing fresh air. Air untainted by Rick's revelation and by their past.

She sprinted to her own room, let herself in, slammed the door and locked it behind her. Racing into the bathroom, she turned the shower on as hard as it would go, needing the sound to muffle her cries.

She didn't make it inside the cubicle, though.

Instead she slid to the floor, lay her head on the cool, tiled floor and let every ounce of hurt and betrayal out in a low, keening wail. She sobbed for her broken marriage, she sobbed for her year of loneliness—complete and utter aloneness, she sobbed because she'd missed Rick so damn much, and she sobbed because they still loved each other. But most of all she sobbed because even though the day had been perfect—right up until Rick's revelation—she couldn't see a way to being with him again.

Chapter Seven

The cocktail party proved to be excruciating. Bianca had to apply heavy makeup to hide the puffiness around her eyes, and she despised makeup. Felt like her face was caked in muck every time she put the stuff on. But even the sweet kiss of the island sun on her cheeks hadn't been adequate to hide the devastation wrought by her earlier breakdown.

If the face paint wasn't bad enough, she'd also slipped on a pair of her highest heels—much to Mack's distaste.

"We're on an island, Bee," Mack had chastised. "Thongs would be too much footwear."

But Bianca had felt so low, she'd needed something to lift her spirits. Anything at all. At least the heels lifted her physically if not emotionally. But the payback to that was her feet were killing her. Every step was an exercise in agony, and sitting down just made her feel low again, so she was forced to stand, grin and bear it.

Then there was the effort involved in avoiding Rick.

She knew she was being stupid. Knew she was acting

like a two-year-old. But she couldn't help it. Her spirit was too raw to face him again today. She was still too vulnerable. Maybe tomorrow she'd listen to him. Maybe. If she squared her shoulders and pretended hard enough that she didn't care, perhaps she'd be strong enough to hear his truths. She owed him that much. She'd refused to listen to him while they were married. The least she could do was show him the respect of listening when they weren't.

For now, she pasted a smile on her face, pretended she was filled with the sparkle and verve she'd left in Brody's bungalow, and did the rounds with a studied ease.

She spoke to every guest there, filled all the women in about the hen's night the next evening and even endured Great Aunt Alberta's lecture about the evils of divorce.

Bianca spent a lot of effort hiding from Rick. She felt his gaze on her all the time. Had caught him staring at her more than once—but maybe that was because she couldn't seem to look away from him all that often. She thanked God her father and Aidan were both built like mountains, because they provided great hiding spots. Every time the intensity of the distance between herself and her almost-ex-husband became overpowering, she stepped behind her brother or father.

She'd have hidden behind Aidan's mate and fellow firefighter, Luke, as well—the guy was almost as big as Aidan—but he was consumed by watching someone else. Someone he hadn't taken his eyes off the whole night: Kennedy, the photographer. Come to think of it, he hadn't even come on over to say hello or give her a hug. Which was odd, because Luke always made time to give her a comforting hug. Of all of Aidan's friends, he seemed to be the one who most understood her pain of the divorce. He was the one who asked almost daily how she was feeling.

She kind of wished he'd give her a hug now, because she hadn't felt this low for a while.

Once again, she lifted her chin high, stuck a smile on her face and had a grand old festive time of it all. But as soon as she could, she slipped away from the party and escaped back to her room. She didn't bother to adjust the lighting once she got back. Didn't want Rick to think she was even there. She simply stripped and climbed into bed alone.

When the knock came on her door, she ignored it.

When Rick's voice filtered through the night air, asking her to open up, she ignored it too. When his declaration of love came again, she blocked her ears. Well, kind of, but she could still hear him vowing to her that it wasn't over between them. That she could run for now, but eventually they would talk.

The last thing she heard before his footsteps told her he'd left was his muffled oath. She had no doubt his hand was twisted in his hair, tugging it in frustration.

Rick may have come back to her bungalow first thing in the morning, but Bianca wouldn't have known. She'd made sure she was out of there at the crack of dawn. First she'd walked the length of the island, watching the exquisite sunrise over the east side, then she'd headed over to the beach, hoping it would be deserted.

It was. Almost. As her feet touched sand, she passed a young woman she recognized from school heading off the beach. Hayley Bryant was a few years younger than Bee, but a close friend of Mack's. Mack had taken a special interest in her and had mentored her for years.

Hayley looked…shell-shocked, and although she tried, she couldn't seem to manage more than a, "Hello, how are you," which suited Bee fine. She wasn't in the mood for chatting to anyone.

She even managed to avoid the only other person on the beach as she slipped into the ocean. Mack's brother stood staring out at the sea, looking even more astounded than Hayley had. If Bee had been in a less pensive state of mind, she might have stopped to give it another thought. But she wasn't. Rick consumed her every thought.

She spent ages in the ocean, first swimming off her frustration and emotion and then treading water as she watched a pod of dolphins frolicking less than a hundred meters away. They hadn't been there when she'd first walked onto the beach, so seeing them while in the water was an extra special treat.

She bet none of them had to deal with their dolphin mates sleeping with other dolphins.

Bianca would have stopped in for brekky at the Secret Cove, the hotel's main dining room, but she had absolutely no appetite—despite her three hours of activity. Instead she grabbed a bottle of water and hightailed it to Kylie's office. As Kylie was a bridesmaid and she the matron—*maid*—of honor, the two had some serious organization to do for tonight.

There the two of them, and Sienna—Mack's other bridesmaid—sat giggling like schoolgirls while they finalized the entertainment for Mack's hen's night. At Bee's request, Kylie had tracked down a stripper on the mainland and was flying him in by helicopter to give Mack a show. Of course he was coming dressed as a firefighter.

Bee couldn't wait for him to show Mack his hose.

The good thing about working with Kylie and Si on this was that if Mack expressed any discontent at the idea of a stripper—which she wouldn't, because seriously, who turned her nose up at a stripper?—Bianca could point a guilty finger at the resort manager and her friend.

Kylie took them into the kitchen to finalize the menu with the chef, and even though Bianca still had no appetite, she couldn't resist stealing one of the millionaire's shortbread slices off the cooling rack. It tasted as decadently rich and delicious as it looked.

She met her parents for lunch, and wisely chose a fresh orange juice and Greek salad, which she nibbled at with disinterest. A part of her—a very large part—hungered for grilled cheese and a glass of red wine.

Then she snuck back to her bungalow, keeping a careful eye out for spare car part shop owners as she went, determined to slip behind trees, shrubs, pools or firefighters if necessary. She still wasn't ready to face Rick.

Her efforts to avoid him came to naught. She couldn't flee from the man who'd settled into a deckchair on her balcony, giving her no option of escape once she'd put her key in the lock.

Her hand shook so badly she couldn't open the door.

Rick helped. He walked over to stand at her back, put his hand around hers and turned the key. Then he opened the door, nudged her so she'd walk inside and followed, shutting out the world behind them.

Trapped.

With the man she loved behind her. So close his breath feathered over her neck. So close the heat from his body surrounded hers, and every breath he took echoed with a loud rasp in her ear. Even the unsteady, jerky breaths.

And regardless of the fact that every cell in her body was conscious of his proximity, of the strain and rigidity in his muscles, she still wasn't prepared for the muttered oath that came from his lips, or his sudden action.

Before she could blink, his hands were on her shoulders, he spun her to face him, and his mouth met hers with demanding fury. He didn't mess around. The instant their lips touched, his opened and his tongue sought entrance. He wasn't backing off, wasn't giving her a chance to refuse him. Powerless to stop him, she gave in.

Then instantly regretted it as his tongue ravaged her defenses, leaving them in tatters at her feet.

One kiss. One stupid, measly, heart-stopping, gut-wrenching kiss, and Bianca melted in a puddle in his arms. What was it about this man that turned her into a whimpering fool any time he neared? Either she whimpered from desire or from hurt or from confusion.

His kiss might be seeking, demanding and feverish, but it was also given in anger. Behind those killer lips, Rick was fast reaching his boiling point. His temper was flaring, his emotions bubbling beneath the surface. His arms trembled as he held her, shaking as they always did when he lost his temper in a big way.

He was angry?

Rick?

The man who'd slept with three other women. Who'd put his penis in someone other than her. He was upset?

No way. No fucking way. It wasn't his right to lose the plot. Wasn't his place to be outraged.

Not when she was so mad, so enraged, so...so... goddamned jealous she could hardly bear to be touched by him.

With all the power she contained, she kicked him. In the shin. As hard as she possibly could. And immediately dropped to the floor as agony shot through her foot.

Shit. Shit, shit, shit.

She wasn't wearing shoes. Not even thongs. She'd taken them off before her swim and forgotten to put them back on.

Balancing on one leg, Rick glared down at her, his shin braced in his hand. "What the fuck — ?"

"Damn it, Rick," she yelled, cradling her foot. "You just broke my fucking toe."

"Me?" He pointed to his chest. "*I* broke your toe?"

If she wasn't so pissed off with him, she might have laughed at the disbelief in his expression. It was almost comical. "No. I think you broke two toes, you bastard."

"You kicked me." His voice was almost as loud as hers.

"Be grateful I didn't knee you in the goolies. That's what you deserve."

He raised an eyebrow. "And what? Once you'd crippled my balls, then you'd have accused me of dislocating your knee?"

She rubbed her throbbing toes. "What are you doing here anyway?"

"What do you think I'm doing here? Tracking you down. Pinning you to one place so that you'll bloody well stick around and talk to me, rather than hiding behind anyone or anything that might be standing between us."

"What if I don't want to talk?" There she was again. The two-year-old Bianca.

"You can't have it both ways, babydoll." He gingerly lowered his leg to the ground, right in front of her, giving Bianca a close-up of the small lump that had formed on his shin. That was going to be bruised by tomorrow. "You can't accuse me of not talking to you enough and then hide when I try to do what you want me to."

She sniffed haughtily. "We're getting divorced. I can do whatever I want, and I don't need your approval anymore." Just like he didn't need her approval for his actions. As soon as they'd decided on the divorce, he'd jumped into the sack with someone else—and he sure hadn't asked for her okay on the matter.

"We're getting divorced because you seemed to believe that was the only solution to our problems. But what if it's not? What if there's another way to sort this out?"

Damn it, did he have to be so tall? When she stood upright she had to crane her neck to look him in the eye. Sitting in this position would likely give her whiplash.

Flipping great. Whiplash and a couple of broken toes. Was it any wonder they were divorcing?

She dropped her gaze back to his injured shin. "We tried every other way. It didn't work."

"No, we didn't." She heard him sigh, heard a rustle of clothes, and then he was sitting on the floor in front of her, his legs crossed. "We gave up on us. Grew apart, accused each other of being strangers and decided strangers couldn't make a marriage work. We never sat down and thrashed out the problems."

She chewed on her lower lip.

"Did we mean so little to you, Bee? Don't our ten years of marriage warrant a little more effort than dusting your hands of us?"

"We meant everything, Rick. Everything. You were my world. My reason for waking up in the morning. So when I woke up one day and realized the man beside me had become a stranger, had turned into someone I no longer recognized, my world fell apart. I spent months waiting for the man I knew to emerge once again from that stranger. He never did." A nasty lump formed in her throat, burning the inside walls. But she wouldn't let the lump reduce her to tears.

"And I spent months looking for an opportunity to talk to you, waiting for the signal that you wanted to talk about us and never found it."

"I asked you to talk to me. I begged you. Repeatedly."

He nodded. "You did. You…." His voice trailed off and he swallowed. "You left Post-it notes on the fridge, saying we need to talk. You left voice messages on my phone while I was at work, saying the same thing. Hell, I even got texts and emails from you pleading for us to sit down. And every time I tried, every time I opened my mouth, you had to make supper or change clothes or send an email or water the garden. Or you were too tired or too hungry or too hormonal, or too aroused. Jesus, Bee, how many times did you silence our conversations with sex? I stopped trying to talk because you wouldn't listen. You didn't want to hear what I was saying, and I didn't want to push you for fear of hurting you."

She dropped her head in her hands, rubbed at her eyes and tried halfheartedly to argue with him. "I listened to you, Rick. Whenever you spoke."

"When I spoke about the small things. About the broken lawnmower or the late payments at the repairs shop or the speeding ticket I got in a school zone. We spoke about the easy-fix situations. We never spoke about us."

Talking about which… "I never knew you hated your work so much."

"I told you about it a few times. Even mentioned wanting

to sell the place once."

Bianca stared at him, askance. He had. He'd mentioned someone had made him an offer and he'd been considering accepting it. But she'd stopped him with a shake of her head. "The steady income is too good," she'd said. "I'm not sure we'll make ends meet without it." And that had been the end of that conversation. She hadn't explored it further with him.

"God." She almost choked on the word. "You must hate me."

He looked at her, appalled. "I could never hate you."

"But I never listened, and I couldn't see that. I kept blaming you for everything. Blaming you for not bringing our problems into the open."

"You frustrated me." He pointed to the side of his head and gave her a half-smile. "I think I have a little bald spot, right there, from tearing my hair out."

It was her turn to swallow. "I'll listen to you from now on. If you have something to say, I'll hear it, no matter how hard it is for me. I just might need you to give me a gentle nudge sometimes. Like when I make excuses, or tell you I'm too busy to talk now."

He nodded, slowly. "I'll take you up on that."

"But…" Oh, God, how did she say this?

"But?"

"But my agreeing to listen doesn't mean our problems are all solved." Oh, no. Not even close. "We still have a mountain standing between us." A volcano, really. One that had erupted on a regular basis over the last few years.

Chapter Eight

Rick's mouth twisted—like it always did when she brought up the mountain. He took a deep, controlled breath. "I know *it's* still there. Separating us. It's not as if I haven't thought about it while we've been apart. Obsessively. But… Before we talk about it, there's something you need to know."

Her heart sank. His tone of voice and the wariness in his eyes sent alarm bells screeching through her head. She kept her expression blank, kept her voice neutral, but inside her belly heaved. "And that is?"

"The women I…" He flexed his hands. "The women I slept with, it wasn't just about sex."

Now her stomach didn't just heave, it turned upside down and inside out, and she was grateful she hadn't eaten more than a couple of lettuce leaves for lunch. Otherwise the contents of her stomach would be dramatically displayed on the floor.

"Jesus, Bee? Are you okay?"

She stared at him wordlessly. No, she wasn't okay. How

could he possibly imagine she'd be okay after what he'd just said? It hadn't just been sex for Rick. The encounters with those women had meant something to him.

"You've turned white." His hands were on her cheeks, his eyes feverish with concern.

She pursed her lips and pronounced each word of her response very carefully. "I promised to listen to you when you spoke to me. That doesn't mean I have to like what you're saying."

He smiled then and sat back in…relief? "But see, that's the thing. You will like it when I tell you. I promise."

She didn't bother responding. The conversation focused on Rick sleeping with other women. At this point she had nothing to say that would do anything positive for their relationship. Nothing at all. So she bit hard on the inside of her cheek and prayed the pain would dull the effect of his words.

"Sleeping with them wasn't just about sex. It was about me discovering what it meant to make love to a woman." His eyes shone with excitement.

Yesterday Rick had told her he'd had sex. Now he was talking about another experience altogether. Making love. *Love*. Not finding a physical release, but discovering a very real, very binding emotion while in the process of having sex.

Bianca swore she felt any remaining color drain from her face. Felt all the blood flow from her cheeks to regions unknown. Maybe it all headed straight to her chest, and that was why her heart beat so damn haphazardly. It couldn't deal with the deluge.

"I learned the difference between the two this year, Bee. Learned that sex and love don't have to go hand in hand. I learned I could fuck someone and feel nothing at all, and I could sleep with someone and feel everything is right with the world. And I learned that I don't want the sex without the love. I don't want a meaningless night in the sack, because it's not enough."

Bianca's heart broke. Just like that. Rick, her husband of ten years, hadn't just had sex with someone else. He'd made love to her. He'd discovered a binding, real emotion in the process and that woman had...had made everything right in his world.

Despite all Rick's promises that he still loved Bianca, he'd made love to another woman.

Now it didn't matter that her heart struggled to beat, because the will to live, to survive another day, eluded her. If she'd struggled to accept the fact that Rick had had sex with other women—which was a purely physical act, then coming to terms with the idea of him making love to someone else almost killed her. She closed her eyes, let the agony consume her, opened them, blinked, tried to focus then closed them again.

When she opened them once more it was to find Rick staring expectantly at her.

Was he waiting for a response? He wanted her to speak? Seriously?

"Er..." She scrambled to think of something, anything. She had to respond, because she'd promised Rick she'd listen. And even though she regretted that decision with every fiber of her being, a promise was a promise. "That's nice?"

"That's nice? That's all you have to say?"

She pasted a lifeless smile on her face. "That's lovely?"

Anger flashed in his eyes. "Jesus, Bianca. Have you been

listening to a single word I've said?"

She nodded. "Of course. You told me that this last year you'd discovered the difference between sex and love, and that you, um, what? Made love to a woman who made everything right in your world?"

His hand twisted in his hair. "That's what you heard?"

"You didn't say that?"

He swore. "No, I didn't say that."

"Do you love her?"

"Who?"

"The woman who made everything right in your world."

"I've always loved her."

Bianca stood. Pain shot through her toes at the movement, but she was barely aware of it. In all fairness to Rick, she'd fulfilled her promise and listened to him. But enough was enough. She didn't have to continue sitting here as he destroyed her life one sentence at a time.

She limped over to the door and held it open for him to leave. "Okay. Well, good. So I guess I'll see you at the wedding?"

"Close the door, Bianca," he whispered dangerously. "We're not finished speaking."

"Yes, we are. You've said enough."

He sprang to his feet. "I haven't said a tenth of what I came here to say."

"The fraction you told me kinda painted the whole picture. I don't need to hear any more."

"You have no idea about the whole picture."

"You fucked three women and fell in love with one of them. Picture complete. Now leave."

He poked her in the ribs with his elbow.

She narrowed her eyes at him. "What are you doing?"

"Giving you that gentle nudge you asked for."

She poked him straight back. "There was nothing gentle about that. And I didn't need it. I listened, I heard, and now you leave. Goodbye."

"I fucked other women."

Tiny spots of red dotted her vision. "So you said. Now get out."

"And not one of them was you."

Dotted? The red almost blinded her. "Yes, I worked that one out on my own, since I wasn't there for any of the momentous occasions."

"You're not listening again. I said I had sex with them. All of them."

"I heard you the first time. And the second and the third. In fact, your words haven't stopped ringing through my ears. Now get the hell out of my room and leave me alone. Forever."

Rick took hold of the door and rammed it, so hard that she lost her grip and it slammed shut. "There is a difference between fucking and making love. A giant ocean of difference. The one is a meaningless act borne of nothing but frustration and the need to come, and the other is an expression of emotion, the ultimate admission that your heart belongs to another person."

Bianca punched him in the stomach with as much force as she possessed.

Then winced as red-hot pain shot through her fingers.

Jesus Christ. His stomach was harder than a freaking rock. What the…? When had that happened?

The breath whooshed out of him, and he grimaced. He grabbed his stomach. "That…hurt." Air hissed from between his clenched teeth, and his eyes squeezed shut.

"Good," she yelled at him. "I hope it continues hurting long into tonight and well into tomorrow and the next day. The next *year*." She shook her hand out, regretting it almost immediately as the red-hot pain knifed back through it. At this rate she'd cripple herself attacking Rick. "Now you know how I feel. Now you know what it's like to be hit by the truth over and over and over again." She clenched her hands into fists, considered smacking him again and decided against it—not for his sake, for hers. "I get it. Okay? I get that you slept with other women. I get that you fucked them. I get that you *made love* with one of them. I. Get. It. I'm not an idiot. You don't have to repeat it."

Rick grabbed her by the waist, lifted her up and pressed her against the wall, jamming her there with his body. It happened in the blink of an eye.

"You get nothing," he snapped. "Not a damn thing. You haven't heard me at all. You may have listened, but you didn't hear."

"Just like you," she screamed. "You may have listened, but you didn't hear a word I said yesterday either. Picking me up? Now? Really?"

God, she was so pissed off, she could kill someone. Rick.

He held his arms away from his body, stretching them wide to show her they were empty. "I'm not holding you now. Not supporting you. I'm trapping you here so you damn well hear me. So my words enter those ears of yours and reverberate through your brain until they make sense." His face was scarlet. Ropes of muscle stood out on his shoulders, and a vein pulsed in his neck. "I *fucked* those women. End of story. I fucked them because I couldn't make love to any of them. Could never love any of them. Could never feel anything for any of them, because every single damned emotion I have is tied up in you. Invested in you. You're the only woman I feel anything for. The only woman I love. The only woman I have ever loved. And you're the only woman I have ever *made love* to. Sex without you means nothing. Nothing! An orgasm with no feeling. An empty release. That's it."

His chest heaved against hers. "I fucked them, and every damn time all I could think about was how much I wished it was you. How much I missed you. How goddamned empty my arms were even while I had a woman with me." His face turned even redder and his nostrils flared, but his breath slowed, as did his words. He spoke more calmly. "Jesus, Bee, I thought it would pass. I thought maybe the second woman I was with would be more meaningful. But I was wrong. My heart was just as hollow. And the third woman? She confirmed what I already knew. *I am nothing without you.* I'm an empty shell." His eyes shimmered, and tears spilled over the edges. "Even the worst days spent with you were better than my best days alone."

Bianca gaped at him.

"I ache for you. I dream about you. I love you. Only you. Every day without you is a study in loneliness, and I… I hate it." His breath seemed to stop. "I don't want to live without you anymore. You're my life."

For the first time, Bianca was left speechless. She couldn't think of a word to say. Her head refused to process everything Rick had told her at any great speed. One sentence at a time, her brain seemed to tell her. It was all it could take.

Trapped between his body and the wall, Bianca hung suspended. She couldn't get away, couldn't escape, but then she wasn't sure she wanted to. She tentatively reached a hand up and wiped away a tear with her thumb. Then she did the same with her other hand. She held his cheeks in her palms, dabbing gently at the tears. Tears he'd shed for her.

And once her hands were there, once his warm cheeks were pressed against her skin, she couldn't seem to pull them away. Couldn't seem to let go of him or stop touching him.

Another tear fell, and this time, rather than use her thumb, Bianca kissed it away, tenderly. Moisture spread over her lips, and when she licked them dry, she tasted salt on her tongue.

"Rick," she whispered. Her Rick. "My…husband." She kissed another tear, tracing its path with her lips. When it reached his mouth, she hesitated, stopping to look at him. Twin oceans of color stared straight back at her, and in his eyes, she saw a reflection of the words he'd spoken. He gazed at her with a sea of love.

Bianca was unaware of where his next tear fell. She was oblivious to everything save that luscious mouth of his, that delicious lower lip. She could no longer resist, no longer wanted to. She pressed her mouth to his and kissed him.

Her lips melded to his, her chest relaxed between the width of his glorious shoulders, and her breasts flattened against his pecs. She wrapped her arms around his neck and melted into him, became a part of him. Her tongue slipped into his mouth, tasting that minty breath again, luxuriating in the slide of his tongue against hers, and when salt mingled with mint, she knew his tears were not the only ones that fell.

Long, heady moments passed before their kiss ended. Before Bianca drew her mouth back so she could fill her lungs with air again. Before Rick rested his forehead against hers, his eyes closed.

His arms were no longer at his sides. As she'd leant in to kiss him, he'd wrapped them around her, holding her close.

"Bee?"

"Mm?"

"Make everything right in my world again. Please."

Her heart pounded, her chest squeezed tight, and a rush of dizziness made her lightheaded.

"Rick?"

"Mm?"

She wound her legs around his waist, hooking her feet together behind his back. "Carry me to bed."

He carried her as though she were the most fragile of flowers. He didn't stop staring at her, his gaze incredulous, as though he couldn't believe she was in his arms, couldn't believe they were together again.

And when he laid her on her bed, she pulled him down on top of her, her feet still linked behind his back. He kissed her again. Kissed her with lips so sweet they made Bee sigh. And ache. And hunger.

She unfastened the buttons of his shirt, shoving the cotton off his shoulders as his tongue seduced her with velvety strokes. Then she fiddled with the tie on his boardies, loosening it enough that she could push the shorts over his beautiful, trim hips. She cupped his arse, loving the heat that emanated from his skin, loving the firm flesh beneath her palms and loving the hard length of his erection nudging against her thigh.

And still he kissed her. As though cherishing every second of it, as though she were more precious to him than gold. And so she returned his kiss, needing it more than she needed air. Needing to keep tasting the mint of his breath, the velvet of his tongue, the silk of his mouth.

Just as she'd so meticulously gotten rid of his clothes, so he'd found a way to unwrap her sarong and free her from her bikini top and bottom. Bianca found herself skin to skin with her husband, the hair on his legs prickly against her smoother thighs, the muscle of his chest a heavenly weight above her breasts and the hard flesh of his cock a burning reminder of why they were here. On her bed. Naked.

Once again she wrapped her legs around his waist, the familiarity of the move both comforting and carnal. Her inner thighs twinged, stiff from overuse. For a year she hadn't slept with a man, and now, for the second time in twenty-four hours, she and Rick were making love.

Warm heat flooded her pussy. Sizzles of anticipation shot up her spine. A low, needy whimper escaped her, and there he was. Rick. Twisting his hips, aligning his groin with hers, the tip of his shaft pressing against her swollen lower lips.

And still he kissed her, hypnotizing her with the sure strokes of his tongue, bewitching her with practiced caresses, wrapping her in his love.

He thrust, slowly, gently, sliding inside her. She opened up to his penetration, her body welcoming him, luring him in deeper, needing him inside her. When he thrust again, seating himself as far as he could go, Bianca felt a bone-deep contentment. A sense of rightness in the world. A sense she'd been without for the last year.

And there it was again. That connection. The soul-deep link to another person. Although, to be fair, she'd felt it since she'd kissed away his tears. It throbbed between them like a living bond. Something so real, she could almost reach out and touch it. But there was no need. Because wrapped around Rick like this, the connection touched her. Touched them both. Held them together in a cocoon of love and understanding.

Rick groaned and stared into her eyes. Held her gaze. And in those eyes she read everything she needed to know. He'd found his rightness in the world too.

He rolled them, landing on his back, with her on top. She didn't hesitate, didn't need to. She knew exactly what he wanted. Bianca rose to her knees, with Rick still buried inside her. She rested her hands on his chest, rocked her hips and rode him. Slow at first, and then harder and faster, taking him deeper with each swivel of her waist, his feral moans egging her on.

Rick's hands found her breasts, caressing them. They swelled in his hands, her nipples puckering tight. Her throaty moan must have touched something in him, because he pulled her down to kiss her, deeply, intimately, his tongue mimicking the thrust of his cock. In this position, with him pressed so close to her, he couldn't drive in as deep as he had been, but his deft strokes teased that knot of nerve endings inside her, sending her to a different level of passion, a needier, desperate one.

She stretched out along his length, and Rick rolled them again, landing on top of her. He took control immediately, pushing up on his hands, his shoulders straining as he arched his back and pumped into her. Sensation sent Bianca spinning in dizzying circles. She bent one knee, inviting him in deeper, and tangled her other leg around his, needing as much contact with him as possible, needing to touch him wherever she could, needing to confirm this was Rick, her husband, making love to her.

Because no matter what those divorce papers said, Rick was her husband. He was her soul mate. He had been for twelve years. Since the first time he'd kissed her at the tender age of sixteen outside her parents' house, Bee had known there could be no other.

She rolled them this time, not far, just so they lay on their sides, pressed against each other. This way, she could slip one arm beneath his neck and free her other hand to touch him. Same with him. And touch her he did. Even as the angle of his thrusts changed completely, so his hand trailed over her side, from her thigh over her hip, brushing the side of her breast and trailing back down again.

She focused on reacquainting herself with the feel of his body. It had changed. Not much, but enough to be noticeable. He'd gotten bigger—slightly more muscular or maybe just harder and more toned. There wasn't an ounce of spare flesh anywhere, which might explain how she'd hurt her hand on his stomach. Before there'd been a hint of a softening around the waist. Not anymore. Now he was lean and muscled and...delicious.

She couldn't remember the last time she and Rick had kissed this intensely, for this long. Towards the end, they'd still had sex, frequently—because she'd never been able to keep her hands to herself when he was around—but they'd stopped kissing as much. That side of their intimacy had dwindled and burned out.

She loved kissing him. Adored it. Lost herself to the expertise of his mouth and lips and tongue. Felt closer to Rick than she had in a very, very long time.

"Bee?" He peppered her face with soft kisses.

"Mm?"

His lips slid exquisitely over her cheeks, her chin, her eyelids. "You're the only one for me. Ever."

"Mmm." Her answer was a purr of exhilaration.

"My world…it's feeling right again."

"M-mine too." More than right. Truth be told, it was tilting on its axis, happiness spiraling through her, desire running rampant and passion just seconds away from exploding.

"Never letting you go again, Honeybee." His thrusts grew intense, hard, deep. "Keeping you in my arms forever."

Right where she wanted to be. Always.

"Love you." He lost his rhythm, pumped into her fast and furiously. "Love you…so damn much."

It was all she needed to hear, all she wanted to hear. The happiness spiraled, the desire expanded and the passion exploded. Bianca came, entwined in the arms of her husband, the man she loved.

Her orgasm spurred his, and he climaxed too. Spilled inside her, a wild, heaving mass of man coming apart in her arms.

She held him as tight as her passion allowed, clinging to him as much as he clung to her. Together their love and their desire and their content sent them over the edge and into a place she'd only ever been with Rick.

Paradise.

Chapter Nine

Bianca lay exhausted on the floor. Rick lay beside her, his arms splayed above his head, his legs stretching out endlessly. Twisted sheets littered the space around them.

He looked at her with a sexy smirk. "Think we set a new record?"

She grinned. "Nah. Remember that night in Sydney?"

A wicked gleam lit his eyes. "Oh, yeah. Impossible to forget. But—" He held up a finger, telling her he was about to make a point. "That was a whole night. And we were years younger. This is just, what, a sunlit afternoon?"

"Maybe," she conceded. "But the truth is, you're way older now. An old fart, really. Bet you can't even get it up again."

Rick nodded sadly. "Bet you're right. But gimme some credit here. I've already come three times in as many hours."

She sniffed proudly. "You may have only come three times. Me? At least five."

"Five?" He raised an eyebrow. "I thought four." His

hand found her thigh and stroked.

"Mmm." She smiled mischievously at him. "I came twice when you went down on me. Only I didn't tell you about the first one, 'cause I didn't want you to stop."

His expression was a mixture of amazement and amusement. "No worries there, Honeybee. 'Cause when I get to tasting your pussy, I never want to stop." His hand slid around so it settled on her inner thigh.

Bianca let her legs drop open, giving him room to brush his fingers over her sensitized skin. "I missed this, Rick."

"I missed you, Bee." He inched his hand higher.

She stared down at his arm. "Subtle moves there, Evans."

"Nothing subtle about my intentions, Rogers. I want to touch you." He traced a finger over her pussy, making her shudder.

She sighed. "Rogers?"

"Just following your lead. That's how you introduced yourself. It's how you registered at the resort." His finger traced over her pussy again, up and down, from her lips to her clit, a feather-light touch that had her tingling all over.

"I tried getting used to being a Rogers again." She stared at her ringless finger.

"And did you?"

She shook her head and spread her thighs a little wider, loving his gentle touch. "I've been an Evans for ten years. I don't remember how to be a Rogers."

"And I don't know how to be just Rick. I'd gotten too used to being Rick and Bee."

"Is that what you want now? To be Rick and Bee again?"

The rhythm of his touch didn't change, a slow, steady seduction of every nerve in her groin. "It's what I've always wanted. What I always will want."

"I want it too."

A long silence followed her admission. A silence filled only with the sensuous strokes of Rick's finger.

"Can I burn them?" he asked finally.

"Burn what?" It was hard to concentrate. Sensation built where he touched her. The tingles increased to shivers, and liquid spilled from her pussy, wetting his fingers. God, she was sticky down there. Full of his come and hers, and she loved it.

"Those fucking papers." For the first time his rhythm faltered. "The ones sitting in my lounge room, taunting me every time I look at them." He inhaled and settled back into stroking her again, gently. "I want to take a match to them and watch them turn to ash."

"I hate them," Bee confessed. "Hate everything they stand for."

"Me too. Every damned thing."

Another lengthy silence followed, one instigated by Bianca. She couldn't have spoken if she'd tried. Pleasure and bliss welled inside her. She dropped her head to the carpet and enjoyed Rick's seductive caress.

At another time she may have twisted her hips, encouraged him to dip that finger inside her. But for someone who hadn't had sex in a year, the last three marathon hours were more than enough for her tender channel. His light caress on her clit and lips was perfect, and she suspected he knew as much.

"Rick…" Her breath caught.

"Mm?"

"I-I'm gonna come."

He growled low in his throat. "Say my name, Bee."

"Hm?"

"I need to hear my name on your lips when you come."

The sensation built, heightened by his demand. "Brody," she whispered.

He growled again. "My real name."

"B-Broderick."

He snorted and stroked her just a little more firmly. "Bianca," he said sternly.

"Rick," she breathed. "Rick Evans." Oh, God. She was close. So close. Could hardly breathe.

"Say your name," he demanded.

"Bee. Bee Rogers."

He shook his head, stilled his hand. "Your real name."

She arched her back, pleading for his touch. "Bianca… Evans."

His face broke into a smile. The corners of his mouth lifted, and even his eyes seemed to grin at her. He gave her what she needed, stroking her pussy again, touching her clit, her lips, caressing her, over and over, soft, gentle torture. Exquisite torture. Perfect torture.

Bianca came. A sweet, beautiful orgasm that rippled through her and left her breathless and happy as sin.

"Can I do it? Bee? Can I torch the papers?"

"Rick." Her sigh was soft. "I *want* to burn them. Want to rip them to shreds first."

"But…"

"But it's not over. We still have to face facts." Sadness overwhelmed her. "It's not as if by admitting we still love each other and want to be married I'll miraculously stop wanting to be a mother."

Rick met her words with silence, which didn't surprise her at all. He'd never wanted children. Never wanted to be a father.

At first, his reasoning had been valid. They were too young, just kids themselves. But they'd grown, matured, and while Bee's need for a family had increased, Rick's hadn't. Not at all. He'd unwaveringly told her he was happy to be the two of them.

"I can change many things about me, about us, Rick. I can force myself to listen or you can make me hear you. I'll let you carry me whenever you want, even learn to enjoy it again. But I can't—I won't—compromise my desire to have a family. I want children. I want lots of them. I want a home full of babies and toddlers and kids and teenagers. I want to be a mom so bad I about cry every time I see a pregnant woman walk past me. And you…you don't want to be a dad, and I…can't live…with that."

And there it was. The massive mountain that neither of them seemed able to scale, sitting between them once again, a bubbling volcano preparing to erupt.

The stripper did show Mack his hose. Every inch of it.

And Mack's response? She lifted her hand up, holding her thumb and forefinger about an inch apart, implying things about the fake firefighter no self-respecting man would ever want implied.

Bianca burst out laughing when the stripper turned to face the rest of the partygoers, his hands spread in a tell-me-it-isn't-so pose.

It definitely wasn't so. Mack had vastly understated his package. The crowd whooped and hooted in ecstasy.

She took a minute to study the rest of his goods as she sipped deeply from her drink. The man had a smoking-hot body. Ripped, tall and built. He was, in a word, gorgeous.

And he did absolutely nothing for Bianca.

Not a thing. Didn't get her motor racing in any way, shape or form.

Because—as she'd acknowledged a million times over since she'd arrived on the island—the only man capable of revving her motor was her husband. The man who for their entire married life had steadfastly refused to be the father of her children. Steadfastly refused to have children. Full stop.

Bianca drained her glass and headed to the bar, stopping in front of yet another gorgeous man. The bartender. Blond hair, blue eyes and a devil-may-care smile. This hunk had rebel plastered all over him. At any other time he would have at least inspired a second glance from Bianca. Tonight all he inspired was another drink order.

The minute he placed the drink before her, she downed it, ignoring the steady rush that came from the alcohol-steeped concoction.

"Finn," she said, "I would love another shtrawberry daiquiri." Since this was the fifth or sixth drink he'd be mixing for her—she'd lost count—she felt she knew him well enough by now to address him by his first name. "And, pleashe, make sure it's a double shot of rum again."

Funny thing about rum. It acted as a definite anesthetic. Numbed her tongue, first of all. And numbed a lot of the pain that racked her chest too. It also made it difficult to think clearly. Which was brilliant, because the last thing Bianca wanted to do was think. First, she'd be forced to think about Rick and motherhood and marriage. And then she'd be forced to acknowledge that the loud whooping emanating from the other side of the room came from none other than Great Aunt Alberta. And that was too much for anyone to deal with, drunk or sober.

Somebody wound an arm around her shoulders and left it there, a pleasing and familiar weight she hadn't expected at a hen's night. Her nose filled with an intoxicating scent — mellow notes of the outdoors and subtle suggestions of man and musk. Mmm, now if she could just bottle that scent, she could keep it beside her bed to sniff at night. And in the morning. And perhaps once or twice during the day as well.

"Finn," she called to the bartender, and when he turned to her she asked, "is it my imagination, or is there a man shtanding next to me?"

Finn set a glass in front of her, filled to the brim with an icy, red mix. "It's not your imagination at all, ma'am. There's a man right beside you, with his arm around your shoulders." He stepped back as if to move away.

"No, wait," Bee stopped him.

Finn looked at her enquiringly.

"Ish…Is," she corrected, "he cute?"

The bartender raised an eyebrow. "Cute?"

"You know," she said conspiratorially. "Good-looking. Shexy. With a lower lip that tashtes…tastes like…" She searched for the right word. "Heaven?"

"Er…" Finn rubbed his hand over his chin. "Yes, ma'am. He's all of those things. Cute, shexy, good-looking. And his lower lip? More a taste of creamy chocolate than heaven, I'd say."

Bianca gasped, horrified. "You've tasted it?"

Before Finn could answer, a voice broke in. "No need to say any more. I'll take it from here."

"No worries, mate. She's all yours." Finn grinned at him. "Nice lip, by the way." And then he was gone, walking away to serve someone else.

Bianca turned to him. "It is a nishe lip," she agreed with

a nod. "Very nishe. Makes me want to nibble on it."

She leaned in and did just that, taking his luscious lower lip between her teeth and nibbling away.

Rick emitted a strangled moan, caught her face in his hand and gently disengaged his lip from her teeth. "Unless you want to explain to every female relative in your family what you're doing with your soon-to-be ex-husband's lip in your mouth, I suggest you stop doing that, now."

Worry besieged her. "Do-do you think they'll want to nibble on it too? What if Finn shpread the word it tastes like chocolate? Which it doesn't, by the way. More like heaven, for sure. But they'll all want a taste anyway." The thought perplexed her, and unsure how to deal with hundreds of family members bearing down on Rick's lip, she sought an answer in her freshly made strawberry daiquiri.

She didn't find an answer there, but she did find a mouthful of something so delicious she took another sip. And another. Finn was a good bartender. No, a great bartender. He hadn't forgotten about the double shot of rum. The alcohol burned a nice little trail of numbness down her throat.

"May I have a sip of that?" Rick asked.

Bianca immediately handed over the glass, chastising herself for not thinking to offer him any. How rude was she?

He took it, set it down on the counter—far out of her reach—and with his hand placed on the small of her back, urged her to walk with him. "Let's go, Honeybee."

But...but she hadn't finished her drink. "Go where?"

"Back to your room."

She glared at him, appalled. "It's Mack'sh hen's night. I can't leave."

"Sure you can. Look, the party's almost over, anyway. Lots of people are leaving. Including the bride-to-be."

Bianca looked up just in time to see her brother whisking Mack out of the room. "Oh. You're right."

"Walk with me?" he asked.

She agreed and let him lead her out into the quiet, balmy night air and across the lush hotel lawn. "I don't shuppose you wanna stop and make a baby on the way?" Struck by inspiration from Mack, she showed him her thumb and forefinger, holding them an inch apart. "Just a little one."

Rick snorted. "You, my lovely wife, are loaded."

She was? "With what?"

"Alcohol. You're drunk."

Oh. Right. She frowned. "Drunk people can still make little babies."

He wrapped his arm around her again, and she leant into it, grateful for the support. She didn't remember walking being quite so complicated before.

"They can indeed," Rick agreed. "But I'm not making a baby while my wife is trashed."

She brightened immediately. "If you bring me a strong coffee, I'll be fine. Then we can make a baby."

"Bee—"

"Just a little one," she hurried to remind him. "A little baby, not a little coffee. I think I'll need a big coffee to do the job."

"A big coffee won't sober you up. Five liters of the stuff wouldn't do the trick."

She sighed. "You're just saying that 'cause you don't want a baby."

"I'm saying that because you're plastered. And as adorable as you are plastered, I'm not prepared to discuss the semantics of you getting pregnant when you can barely put one foot in front of the other."

"Oh." Disappointment engulfed her. "You noticed?" She thought she'd done a good job of hiding her unsteadiness.

"Me and everyone else on the island."

"Rick?"

"Yeah?"

"Would it be okay if you carried me the rest of the way? I, er, don't think I can make it back to my room on my own two feet."

He placed a tender kiss on her forehead. "I think it would be very okay."

Chapter Ten

Bianca awoke to sunlight blazing through her window and Rick standing beside her with a bottle of water.

"Rise and shine, sleepyhead. You've got a big day ahead of you, and it's already noon."

Bee bolted upright and immediately wished she hadn't. Pain streaked through her head, making her wince.

Rick uncapped the bottle and handed it to her, along with two white pills. "Panadol. I figured you'd need them this morning. Make sure and drink all that water. We need to rehydrate you before the wedding."

The wedding! It was a few hours away, and she wasn't ready. She dutifully downed the pills with some water, grateful to have Rick there looking after her. Then she made her way slowly to the bathroom where she brushed her teeth and washed her face.

The glare from the sun made her squint as she gingerly picked her way back to bed. "You spent the night here last night."

He'd spent the night cuddled against her back, and she'd relished each second of it.

Rick closed the blinds, providing instant relief. "I plan to spend every night with you from now on." He sat on the edge of the bed. "You're my wife, Bee. We need to be together. I think we established that pretty effectively yesterday."

It was only when his mouth tilted upwards that she realized he was staring at her chest. She looked down to find herself naked from the waist up. All she wore was a pair of panties.

She pulled the sheet up around her breasts tentatively. Hasty movements were murder on her head. "All we established yesterday was that we love each other and still want to be married. We didn't actually resolve the key problem."

"That's because you didn't give me time. You had to hurry out and help Kylie with the party. If you'd hung around a little longer we could have sorted it out there and then."

She took another long sip from the bottle. Her shoulders heaved with a huge, despondent sigh. "How do we resolve this? How do we find a middle ground between you not wanting to have children and me wanting a whole heap of them?"

There really was no solution. None at all. She tried not to let the hopelessness overwhelm her again.

"How about we start with one child and take it from there?" Rick asked.

Bianca froze mid-blink. She couldn't open her eyes. Couldn't breathe. "I-I'm sorry. What did you say?"

"I said, let's start by having one child, and see how things work out from there."

"You...um..." She had to clear her throat to speak. "You want to have a child? You...you'd have a baby with me?"

He took her hand in his, held it so tenderly tears welled in her eyes. "Do you have any idea how many nights I spent alone this last year?" He shook his head. "Too many. No one should have to endure that kind of forced isolation. It's a killer."

Bianca didn't want to talk about loneliness or nights by himself. She wanted to focus on the real issue. "Rick…"

"It gave me time to think. Plenty of time. To realize what I missed and what I wanted most in my life. I missed *you*. I missed my wife and my best friend. I missed the woman who makes me whole. I wanted her back. And the more I thought about that, the more I came to understand there was only one thing that could be more fulfilling than having you back in my life. And that would be having two yous in my life."

She gulped, barely able to believe what she heard.

"I never wanted children before, because you gave me everything I needed. You alone were enough for me to be happy. And if I'm honest, I was scared to share you with someone else. Selfishly scared. But now I can see that I'd still have you if we had a child. I'd just have more. I'd have you and our baby. I'd have two of you, and that…that…" For a long moment he couldn't talk. "That wouldn't just make me happy. That would fill up my life in ways I never imagined possible. I couldn't have imagined it before, because I didn't know what it felt like to be so truly alone."

"You-you have to know that more than anything in life, I want to have your baby, Rick. I want us to be a family and not just a couple."

He nodded. "I've always known that, and now I understand it too. It's what I want as well. But…"

"But?"

"I can see a baby in our future. One, maybe two. But the idea of a whole houseful of kids…" He grimaced. "I'm not there, Bee. I'm not sure I can deal with that."

She shook her head. "That's okay by me. That is so okay. We can start with one. Just one, and take it from there. I'll be happy with two or three or ten, but if one is all you can cope with, I'm good with that." As long as she had a baby, Rick's baby, to hold in her arms, she'd be okay. Because if she had Rick and she had a child, she'd have a family. She'd have what she'd yearned for, for so long.

"I'm good with two." He smiled, and the smile was more dazzling than any sun could ever be.

"I'm good with you." She smiled too. "I'm better with you than I ever was on my own."

"Just promise me neither of us will ever have to be on our own again, and I'll be happy."

"Neither of us will ever have to be alone again," she told him. "Not ever."

And that was all he let her say, because his mouth was on hers, and he was kissing her, and words were not necessary again for a very long time.

Bianca kicked off her shoes as she walked onto the beach. The sand was warm, but not hot enough to burn her feet as she'd feared. Besides, she didn't need the heels to feel a hundred feet tall. She just needed Rick. And now that she had him again, she was tall enough to touch the clouds.

She glided down the makeshift aisle with Kylie and Sienna beside her, grinning as she saw her brother up ahead, a look of sheer happiness on his face. She knew he didn't see her. He searched only for the woman walking behind her in a simple white shift dress. The perfect dress for a beach wedding.

Bianca scanned the seats, seeking out one person. She found him easily. He was the one gazing back at her with an ocean of joy in his eyes. His smile broadened as their eyes met, and she wondered if she'd ever felt this happy or content. The only day she could think of that might equal this one was her own wedding day.

Rick sat a few seats down from the aisle, making it difficult for Bianca to give him the gift she'd brought for him. But that didn't stop her. She paused to whisper in the ear of her second cousin, who sat on the edge of the same row as Rick, and handed the gift to her, asking her to pass it on.

The woman looked confused but handed it to her husband beside her. Bee continued up the aisle until she stood close to Aidan. While every person at the wedding stood and turned to watch the bride walk over to meet her groom, Bianca turned to face her husband.

Two days ago, she'd been determined to return home and finally sign her name to those damned divorced papers. Now instead of picking up a pen, she and Rick could destroy the pages together.

Rick stood by his seat with a bemused smile on his face. In one hand he held the small box she'd found for him, the box where she'd carefully printed the words, *Go ahead. Burn them.* In the other he held a match that he'd taken out of the box.

As their gazes caught and held, Rick struck the match, and together they watched the flare of a flame that promised to burn away every last barrier to their happiness.

About the Author

Once Jess Dee discovered it was okay to leave the bedroom door open in her romance novels, she decided to leave everything open. Buttons, zips, pants, number of lovers… Which is why her books are all steamy erotic romances.

While Jess lived most of her life in South Africa, the last thirteen years have been spent in Australia. From the fast paced Sydney lifestyle to the laid back islands and beaches, there's always another gorgeous Aussie setting for a contemporary romance.

Enjoy the entire Bandicoot Cove series...

PARADISE FOUND
by Vivian Arend

TROPICAL SIN
by Lexxie Couper

ISLAND IDYLL
by Jess Dee

SUNLIT SURRENDER
by Jess Dee

SUNSET HEAT
by Lexxie Couper

MOONLIGHT MIRAGE
by Sami Lee

Other books by Jess Dee

PLANNED SEDUCTION
The Seduction Series

CHANCE SEDUCTION
The Seduction Series

STEVE
Circle of Friends Series

TYLER
Circle of Friends Series

SUMMER WINE
Days of Wine and Roses

RED RED WINE
Days of Wine and Roses

KISSES SWEETER THAN WINE
Days of Wine and Roses

ISLAND IDYLL
Bandicoot Cove

SUNLIT SURRENDER
Bandicoot Cove

WINTER FIRE
Fire

HIDDEN FIRE
Fire

GOING ALL IN
Three of a Kind

RAISING THE STAKES
Three of a Kind

FULL HOUSE
Three of a Kind

MORE THAN FRIENDS
More Than This

MORE THAN LOVERS
More Than This

Visiting paradise

The One That Got Away

ONLY FOR A NIGHT
a *Lick* novella by Naima Simone

Rion Ward fought hard to be free of the Irish mob life. Now, as the co-owner of Boston's hottest aphrodisiac club, he's traded crime for the ultimate sexual fantasy. When Harper Shaw, a good girl from his past, walks through Lick's doors, he discovers that his unconsummated hunger for her never abated. He'll be hers only for one night. One night to explore her every fantasy. One night to push her limits. One night to introduce her to a passion that makes both doubt if it will be enough…

TEMPTING HER NEIGHBOR
a *Small Town Temptations* novel by Laura Jardine

Tired of big city life, software developer Cole Sampson moves to a small Canadian town to get some peace and quiet. Unfortunately, his keep-the-hell-away-from-me vibes don't work on his gorgeous new neighbor. And she's determined to win him over…

Made in the USA
Middletown, DE
01 December 2017